T0313502

MARY
PRINCE

E. L. NORRY

■SCHOLASTIC

To the lightbringers x

Published in the UK by Scholastic, 2022
1 London Bridge, London, SE1 9BA
Scholastic Ireland, 89E Lagan Road, Dublin Industrial Estate, Glasnevin,
Dublin, D11 HP5F

SCHOLASTIC and associated logos are trademarks and/or
registered trademarks of Scholastic Inc.

ISBN 978 07023 1382 0

A CIP catalogue record for this book
is available from the British Library.

Printed by CPI Group (UK) Ltd, Croydon, CR0 4YY
Papers used by Scholastic Children's Books are made
from wood grown in sustainable forests.

1 3 5 7 9 10 8 6 4 2

While this book is based on real characters and actual historical events, some
situations and people are fictional, created by the author.

Any website addresses listed in the book are correct at the time of going to
print. However, please be aware that online content is subject to change and
websites can contain or offer content that is unsuitable for children. We advise
all children be supervised when using the internet.

www.scholastic.co.uk

In the beginning, there was friendship and fun and frolics. But hindsight is remarkable – we do not know what we do not know until our eyes are opened to the way of this world.

Chapter 1

Devonshire Parish, Bermuda

1799

"I'll count to twenty!" Betsey cried, excited, as she let go of my hand. "And then, ready or not, I'll come to find you!"

"I know, I know!" I replied, laughing as we ran down the long corridor towards the front door.

I knew exactly where Betsey wouldn't come looking because it was too dark, and spiders and beetles scuttled and scurried across the floor. I'd seen them when I'd gone to fetch wood. They did not bother me; I liked watching their little legs move so rapidly, wondering where they were going and what they were doing, but scurrying creatures made Betsey squeal. That's how I knew she wouldn't dare venture into the dark, damp barn – so that's where I decided to go.

"I'm a very good seeker," Betsey said, as she tossed her golden ringlets and poked me gently in the belly. "Watch out!"

I squealed and squirmed away from her bony fingers. "You won't find me!"

Betsey howled with laughter as I threw open the door and ran onto the lawn, past the big oleander bush with its vivid pink flowers. I breathed in deeply – June meant there were flowers everywhere, and Betsey and I would often sit and thread them into each other's hair. It was midday and the sun blazed in the cloudless sky.

I followed the house's long, white walls, which gleamed in the morning sunshine. My mother was sorting laundry outside the kitchen and when she glanced up, shielding her eyes against the sun, I waved. She gave a nod and a small smile, then went back to folding the bundles around her. I headed round the side of the house to the barn.

Safe inside, panting, I closed the wooden door.

Betsey will never find me here! I thought to myself, my heart beating fast. How long would she keep looking?

Betsey was eleven years old, the same age as me. She wore beautiful dresses, unlike the drab sack-type dresses I had to wear, and her hair was neat and curled into ringlets; her stiff, starched pinafore was so white that just looking at it hurt my eyes. Betsey loved to hold my hand; we did everything together. We were as close as sisters, but we were not. I had sisters of my own – two in fact, and I was the eldest – but I played more with Betsey than with either of them.

Sometimes Betsey and I had such fun, dancing, singing and twirling all day long, but at other times I was tired, sleepy or hungry and not in the mood to play. But that didn't matter – if Betsey wanted to play, we played. It was not up to me. Not much was.

"Molly!" Betsey's high, sweet voice pierced the air. "Ready or not … I'm coming, Molly!"

Betsey called me Molly, although that's not my name. Betsey preferred Molly, and she could choose what she wanted to call me.

My name is actually Mary, Mary Prince. Sometimes, at night when I'm all alone, I whisper, "*I am Mary!*" to myself, over and over. I do it in case I forget – it's all too easy to become what other people believe you to be; you need to keep reminding yourself of who you truly are.

All was calm and quiet as I sat nestled among the damp, sweet straw, breathing in the smell of the farm animals. I shivered as I realized that, for once, no one had any idea where I was. I could be anywhere. I was hidden. There were no eyes on me and no one to tell me what to do, where to go, or how to behave. I wasn't sure that this had ever happened before. It was a new experience and I liked it. Even though it was sunny outside, the darkness of the barn felt comforting, almost as if it were holding me and keeping me safe.

When Betsey called out again, her voice had changed. All the lightness was stripped from it; she was becoming impatient. That meant I had hidden long enough. I needed to come out and make myself known.

"*Molly!*" The sharp way she said my name told me I should go out to her immediately – she wanted to play. But I was tired, more tired than I had realized, and part of me longed to stay exactly where I was. We had been playing all day: dolls and sewing and tea parties and … it was so peaceful in the barn. My mind had room for my own thoughts when I didn't have to take Betsey's into account. But another part of me, the part that knew my duty was more important than my wishes, urged me to get up and join Betsey.

Mother says we all have a duty. A place in this world. *I* had a duty and that duty was to yell, "I'm here, Betsey!" But still, I said nothing. I stayed as deep and dark and silent as the air around me, imagining that for just one moment, I could be allowed to forget who and where I was, what my duties were – and who I belonged to.

But something strange happened: the longer I stayed quiet, the harder it became to speak at all. I could not unstick my lips from one another, and my throat felt scratchy and swollen, tightening as if hands were squeezing it. There was a hot, prickling feeling behind my eyes. I had the very strong feeling, a fear almost, that if I didn't speak in the very next moment then perhaps I would never find the will to speak ever again…

Footsteps. But instead of Betsey's usual skipping or jumping, these steps dragged and stomped. She was frustrated, getting in one of her moods. She wasn't bad-tempered very often; usually we were both sunny and happy when we were together.

I squinted through the narrow slits in the door and glimpsed flashes of her yellow dress and flapping petticoats.

"Molly?" she asked, her voice wobbling, a sign that tears would soon arrive.

I didn't want to take the blame for Miss Betsey's tears.

"I'm in here!" I bellowed, unscrambling myself and clearing my scratchy throat. Walking out of the dark barn, I squinted into the sunshine.

Betsey's usual smile was now a scowl; her thin, pale arms were folded tightly over her chest. She peered over my shoulder, narrowing her eyes at the swinging barn door.

"That's not fair, hiding in there," she said, wrinkling her nose. "A dirty, dark, smelly barn where animals lie down is no place for a young lady."

She was not being mean on purpose, but by saying "young lady", words that described her but not me, she was making the difference between us very clear.

"I suppose not, Miss Betsey," I said, curtseying low, hoping to soothe her anger. She stared at me, unsmiling, her blue eyes steady and unblinking. Eventually, after a long moment, a little smile curled at the edge of her lips. I knew I was forgiven, her irritation forgotten.

"But you're a slave, Papa says," she continued. "*My* slave, so I s'pose a slave might think a barn is a good place to hide."

"Yes, Miss." I curtseyed even lower, bending my head towards the ground.

"But, Molly," Betsey pressed her lips together – her voice a warning, her smile an instruction. "I forbid you to go in there again."

"Yes, Miss."

And in an instant, Miss Betsey was all sunny smiles and darling dimples again. She scooped up my hand and stroked it. She yanked me this way and that across the gardens, her golden ringlets bouncing in the Bermuda breeze. Our fingers interlinked, my black fingers next to her white fingers like piano keys, as I tried to hold on to that wonderful peace and sense of myself that I had discovered as I sat quiet and alone in the barn.

Chapter 2

Devonshire Parish, Bermuda

1799

"Girls!" called Mrs Williams, Betsey's mother. "Come and eat!"

Mrs Williams was a gentle, kindly woman, and I was very fond of her. She always treated my mother, brothers, sisters and me more as if we were members of her family than her property. With her, it was easy for us to forget that our lives were not our own. It was Captain Williams, the master, who was the fly in the ointment. Thankfully, he was often away from the house for long stretches of time.

Betsey and I sat on a blanket spread out on the lawn outside the kitchen. As we ate our sweet cornbread with molasses and milk, a brilliant red songbird hopped along the branches of the tree that was shading us. As I stared at the shiny, black feathers around its throat, I thought about how lucky I was. Betsey Williams was kind to me, although there was no doubt about my position in the household. I was Betsey's plaything, a living, breathing doll. And I never questioned my position because, in those days, I was happy. In my mind, I had a good life; I was fed and watered and cared for.

One of my favourite things to do was linger among the many books the master kept in his study. Whenever he went away, Betsey and I would play "teacher and student", surrounding ourselves with huge, dusty volumes. Even though back then I couldn't read, I sensed the importance of all the squiggles on the page. I understood that the master's books contained wonders and knowledge, as did the maps on the walls, which showed the different places he travelled to.

Although my mother, my brothers Brown and Yorick, my sisters, Hannah and Dinah, and I all lived together, my father did not live with us. I only got to see him occasionally. He was owned by the Trimmingham brothers and worked in their shipbuilding yard near Crow Lane. My mother, siblings and I had been bought from Mr Myners by old Captain Darrell; Betsey was his granddaughter, and what a fine gift for her I made!

Hannah and Dinah were both younger than me, and although they sometimes got under our feet when Betsey and I were playing, I loved the way they would come and hug me whenever they passed, and Hannah was always eager to show me the latest trinket she'd found.

Betsey's father, Captain Williams, owned a trading ship that carried goods. He was often away, travelling between America and the Caribbean Islands. It was lucky that he was away so often because he seemed to be a very bad-tempered and disagreeable man. Mrs Williams and Mother were always more likely to laugh and smile together when he was away on his travels.

Sometimes when he returned home, he would sit Betsey on his knee and tell her stories of his adventures. Often, as I waited outside the room in case Betsey called for me, I would press my ear against the door to listen. My heart would swell when I heard the captain's tales of stormy seas and the discoveries he'd made. I would close my eyes and imagine that I could smell the sugar or tobacco as it was loaded and unloaded from the ships, and see the amazing sea creatures that followed his ship. I promised myself that, one day, I would go and see those faraway places for myself.

Betsey wasn't very interested in her father's seafaring stories. She was always much more interested in the presents he brought back with him.

"What have you brought me, Papa?" she would ask, her eyes gleaming. Then she'd squeal and giggle as he produced silk fabrics, dollies and foodstuffs so fancy that they made my face glow just to look at them!

I often thought that if he were my father, I would want to go with him on those big ships, sailing the seas and having adventures. Devonshire Parish was my whole world, but I'd seen the globes and maps in the captain's study – and I knew there was so much more world out there.

Our house was down a little lane, very near the sea; on stormy nights, I knew that the bangs and crashes I heard were waves slapping against the breakers on the shore. As I lay awake, I would imagine what an adventure it would be to sail the six hundred miles to the Americas!

My life of amusing Betsey was all I knew; I had no idea that another way of living was possible. I didn't know that I was soon going to discover how big and cruel the world could be.

One day, when Betsey had been called inside, my mother came to sit beside me. She leaned down and touched the back of my neck with her fingers, which were warm from the sun.

"Things gonna change soon round here, little one."

I looked into her big, dark eyes; she sounded more serious than I'd ever heard her. Serious and weary.

"How are they going to change, Mother?" I murmured.

"The captain … I hear only whispers, but it seems his business is suffering. I don't think the money is coming in like it used to."

I felt confused, but Mother carried on, gently: "Mrs Williams has had to sell some furniture and jewellery. She hasn't admitted it, but when I clean the house, I've noticed that more and more objects are disappearing." She clutched her hands to her chest. "I'm afraid that you may be sent away."

"Away?" Cold gripped my heart.

Mother looked down. She bit her bottom lip, and I knew it was to keep it from trembling.

"You are the eldest. You are strong, sensible and obedient. You're a quick learner and that is a prized thing for a…"

The words dried in her throat. I tried to picture a different house, another kitchen, another Betsey – but I couldn't.

I swallowed the tears rising in my throat.

"Where will I be sent?" I stuttered.

"Hopefully not far, little one. Mrs Williams will hire you out; this means that she still owns you, and the money you earn from the work you do will be sent back here, to help her."

"But if Mrs Williams needs money, why doesn't she sell us?"

My mother smiled and said, "Even though Mrs Williams owns me, our relationship has been long and happy. She and I are more like companions, and with the captain away so often, for such long stretches of time, she knows that she can rely on me. Splitting up my family would break her heart as much as it would mine."

I couldn't hold back any longer. I howled as tears rushed down my cheeks.

"Shhh!" Mother stroked my cheek until my sobs died down. "Smile! Keep those tears inside; you mustn't show these feelings. We are expected always to be silent and strong."

I sniffed and wiped my nose on my arm. "If I am sent away, will I still see you?"

She shook her head. "I don't know yet how it will work; I only know that you have come of age and are old enough to work. So you need to be brave and strong, and make Mrs Williams and me proud. No fuss, no tears. Do as you are told with good grace. Trust in the Lord to take care of us."

White people owned us Black people – that was the way of our world. They decided everything, and we obeyed.

Mother was right. A few days later, I waved a tearful goodbye to Betsey as I stepped onto the horse and cart that was to take me to my new position.

"This won't be goodbye!" Betsey cried.

Remembering what mother had told me, I tried to keep my feelings inside, but I couldn't help myself. Hot tears streamed down my cheeks.

Mrs Williams held Betsey close. "Betsey is right, dear Molly, it's not a final goodbye. Betsey is friends with Fanny, the Pruddens' daughter, so you will see her again soon."

"Perhaps we'll see you at church too," added Mother.

We were allowed to attend church if we used the Black entrance; I had only been once or twice, but ever since Mother had heard the Irish missionary Reverend John Stephenson speak, she had become fervent about the Lord's work.

Mrs Williams nodded. "Whenever Mrs Prudden allows you a leave of absence, you are always welcome to come and visit us."

But the Paget parish, where the Pruddens lived, was five miles away – it might as well have been the other side of the world! The truth was, I didn't know when I would see Betsey – or my family – again.

Chapter 3

Paget Parish, Bermuda –
Prudden and Williams Households

1800

At only twelve years old, even though I was still a child myself, I was told that my job would be to look after the new Prudden baby boy, Daniel.

I was about to have my own living, breathing doll. Daniel was a good-natured baby, and for that I was glad. He cooed and babbled, and I carried him on my hip while I did my other tasks. At times I helped Patricia, the cook, to prepare meals, but I made the beds, washed the dishes outside in the yard and worked in the gardens, too. I also helped to grow vegetables on the provision ground, a nearby piece of land that had been given over to the slaves. The soil there wasn't good enough to grow sugar cane, so we grew squash and corn for ourselves.

Being at the Pruddens' wasn't as awful as I feared, though

of course I missed my family and Betsey terribly. There were days when I felt sorry for myself, but I was usually too busy to think much about home. I now realized just how lucky I'd been, living with Betsey and having the "job" of being her playmate.

As I grew older, I took pride in carrying out my tasks well. I was happy knowing that the money I earned was helping both Mrs Williams's and my family to survive. That made me feel very proud.

My days fell into a pattern. In the mornings after feeding Daniel, making the beds and cleaning the house, I would dig for yams and sweet potatoes in the garden. This task was always best done before the midday sun became too hot.

As well as Daniel, the Pruddens had two other children: Miss Fanny, who was my age, and her older brother James. In the afternoons, the three of us would stroll to the beach and dip baby Daniel's tiny toes into the sea. We would laugh as we watched him squeal and giggle. He really was the sweetest, plumpest baby you ever did see. Fanny would sit in the shade of a tree, or she and James might skim stones or collect driftwood and pink conch shells. Although James and Fanny weren't as fun as Betsey, we all got along well enough and I had no cause to complain. I settled into life just fine at the Pruddens'.

One morning as I was hoeing weeds in the garden, Miss Fanny bounded up to me.

"You're so lucky that you don't have to have lessons," she moaned. "I don't want to sit in there, reciting things, when I could be out here playing with you."

I stopped hoeing to rearrange my osnaburg dress. In the heat, the rough, thin fabric prickled my skin and made me itchy. In those days, whenever I dreamed of what it would be like to be a white girl, the first thing I thought of was being able to wear fine clothes in soft, silky fabrics. We slaves couldn't choose what to wear. I once asked Mother why all our clothes were made from osnaburg. She explained that it was cheap and hardwearing, saving the slave owners money. It didn't matter to them that it was so uncomfortable and scratchy! Fanny's and Betsey's dresses had bows and ruffles and were made from silky material that rustled when they walked. But the girls often complained their dresses were itchy and uncomfortable too.

Turning to Miss Fanny, I replied, "Think of how lucky you are!"

She wrinkled her nose. "What do you mean? How am I lucky?"

"I would love to know all that you are being taught,"

I said, thinking of all the books and maps in Captain Williams' study.

She tossed her hair. "Really? Well, if you actually enjoy learning, I've got an idea," she said. "Grandmamma keeps scolding me because my mind wanders and I forget my lessons, but perhaps you could help me."

She told me how she had been learning about the American Revolution and how the Americans had thrown off British rule. I did not say anything, but I was burning to understand more – if an entire country could be made free, then why not us, a few thousand slaves? There and then, with the sun beating down on us, I vowed to learn all I could, so that I could understand my own situation and that of others too.

"If you tell me what you're supposed to remember, maybe we could recite your lessons together," I suggested.

Miss Fanny thought for a moment. "Yes! That sounds a grand idea. I've only just been permitted to have spelling lessons. Today Grandmamma said that 'R-U-N' spells run." She jumped for joy.

"R-U-N," I repeated. "Run!"

Miss Fanny smiled, her dimples dancing. She drew shapes in the air with her finger. Faintly, we heard her mother calling her name.

"And this is how 'R-U-N' *looks*!" she cried gaily, as she sprinted off. She called over her shoulder, "I'll fetch Daniel and then we can take him to the sea." I nodded and carried on hoeing. In my head I chanted "R-U-N" and smiled to myself.

R-U-N. Oh! How I liked to run. How the pounding of my heart against my chest made me feel like I was flying, like I could do anything, go anywhere. Even though I knew this was not true, it *felt* true. It felt … possible. And if feeling a thing was possible, then perhaps one day *being* that thing could happen too.

Through helping Miss Fanny, maybe I could learn to read and write a few simple words myself. The world would open up to me, for me. Hope could creep into my life – hope that, one day, things might change.

"Where is your father then?" Miss Fanny asked me one afternoon at the seashore. James was spinning the baby round. I craned my neck to watch a huge, long-winged seabird fly overhead, making a high-pitched wailing noise as it passed over.

"He works for men who own a sugar plantation." I thought about the last time I had seen my father, many months ago. I watched him sawing yellow-wood timbers under the sun as I stood and breathed in the trees' fragrant aroma. It made me proud that he was so strong and capable, though I wished that I could sit on my father's knee and listen to his stories, like Betsey did with her father. Still, whenever we did see each other, he always had time for a smile and an encouraging word. He would tell me how well I was doing and remind me to take care of Mother, to be respectful – and to make him proud.

"He helps them make their boats," I said, proudly. I knew, from listening to Captain Williams, that the boats sailed to America.

"Today's word is 'B-O-A-T'," Fanny said. She knelt in the sand and with her finger drew the letters. "Now, repeat after me so that I can be sure you have remembered the letters."

"B-O-A-T," I said slowly.

After the lesson, Fanny told me a terrible story that had been passed down through generations, of Sally Bassett, a Bermudian slave who was burned at the stake for trying to murder her owners. I listened to the tale with wide eyes, fear striking my heart at such gruesomeness, but Fanny just laughed and said, "It's good that you're happy here and that history won't be repeating itself!"

She ran off to splash in the water with James. I sat Daniel on my knee and tickled his sweet little toes while I traced the deep grooves her fingers had made as they formed the letters.

"B-O-A-T." I sighed. "One day ... I will travel on a boat."
I nuzzled Daniel's little ear, dreaming of future voyages, smooth seas, splashing waves and faraway islands. Islands where I could live and be free.

When Fanny came back and sat under a tree in the shade, she turned to me and asked, "Do you remember the word I learned today?"

"Boat," I said.

"You *did* remember!" Miss Fanny clapped her hands together, pleased. "James said you wouldn't."

I enjoyed knowing how the words we spoke were spelled, and how to read them too. It was as if they became special treasures that I held close when I had nothing else of my own. At night I would stare at the ceiling and whisper the words Fanny and I had learned: "*Run, boat, table, tree...*"

As I lay awake, I would remember the stories Fanny told me that she'd heard her Grandmamma read aloud from the *Bermuda Gazette* and the *Weekly Advertiser*. Stories about the excitement on the island over the Royal Naval dockyard being built and the wealth that would bring in.

One day, after the sun had cooled and James and Fanny had chased each other back up to the house, I stayed with baby Daniel, listening to the waves lap the shore. I sang to him and fed him some sweet treats. Soon, he was asleep in my arms.

I started to walk along the shoreline, around the inlets and bays, and before I knew it, I'd wandered so far that I was closer to Mrs Williams's house than the Pruddens'. I knew that I'd be welcome to visit, but before I could walk up the path to the house, to my horror, I saw people carrying a body covered by a sheet out of the door.

With baby Daniel still asleep in my arms, I rushed up to the slaves, including my own mother, brothers and sisters, who had gathered by the door.

"What's happened?" I cried. "Who has been taken ill?"

"It's dear Mrs Williams," my mother wept, twisting her hands in front of her. "She was ill, and the Lord has taken her!"

My mother threw her arms around me, pulling me close. We both wept for poor, kindly Mrs Williams. Betsey rushed out of the house to join us.

"My Mama!" she wailed.

I hugged Betsey. It was good to be in the arms of my friend; we both loved Mrs Williams and were united in our grief. That sad afternoon, there was no division between slaves and masters or mistresses.

Later, after our tears had dried, Mother and I sat in the kitchen. She looked fondly at baby Daniel sitting in my lap, while I drank some milk and told her about life at the Pruddens'.

"They are quite fair to me," I told her.

"Why did she decide to let you visit us today? Maybe she heard from her friends at church that Mrs Williams was ill?"

Cold fear shivered up and down my spine.

I gulped. "Mother, I didn't ask her permission to come here today," I admitted. "I … I was just walking on the shore, then before I knew it, I was here. It was as if something was pulling me here to see you all – it felt like so very long since we'd been together…"

"Oh, Mary!" My mother's hand flew to her mouth. "You must go back immediately! Mrs Prudden will be fretting about Daniel, and you will be in trouble for not asking her permission."

"What have I done wrong?" I pleaded.

My mother shook her head, her usual wide smile gone, her mouth a thin line. "You may not have been thinking straight … but you know that you are now someone else's property, my love. Mrs Prudden is your mistress. She can tell you what to do and when. You cannot answer back, you must do everything she asks of you with good grace and utmost obedience, or she is within her rights to punish you. You should leave now – and hurry, so that your punishment may not be so harsh."

"Punishment?" I wondered what to expect. In the twelve

years of my life so far, I had never given my masters any reason to punish me.

My mother turned her face away. "So far you have been protected from seeing how ruthless our masters can be. We were so lucky with Mrs Williams." Her voice was low and sad as she continued, "But there are owners who beat slaves – with a horsewhip or a long, thin tree branch called a switch. Some slaves are struck so hard that they are left with cuts and scars all over their body."

I had never been struck. I couldn't believe the words coming from my mother's lips. Fear thundered around my body and split my very soul. Of course, I had heard slaves get shouted at, but the thought of anyone being struck was truly frightening. Didn't the Bible preach kindness to all people? How could it be that one human being was allowed to hit another? How could inflicting physical pain solve anything?

"When Mrs Prudden asks where you have been, make sure you tell her the truth," my mother said, firmly. "And give her the news about Mrs Williams, if she doesn't already know."

I kissed everyone and reluctantly said my goodbyes before my long, weary walk back to the Pruddens' house. Daniel felt as heavy as a rock in my arms as we walked through the door. What would Mrs Prudden say – or do – to me?

Chapter 4

Paget Parish, Bermuda –
Prudden Household

1800

Mrs Prudden was, as Mother had predicted, very angry. Before she even said a word, her tightly crossed arms and pinched-together lips told me that she was displeased. Despite the afternoon sun, a chill sneaked up the back of my neck.

She snatched baby Daniel from my arms and handed him to the cook. Gripping me by my sleeve, she dragged me into the study.

"Hold out your hand," she demanded. She could not look at me and although her voice was cold, it shook.

"Please, Mistress…" I begged. I sensed a darkness roiling within her; the air was charged with menace.

In her hand, Mrs Prudden held a long, thin switch.

My stomach lurched as I tried to imagine how it would feel to be struck with it. Would it be as painful as that time after the rains when I was chasing Miss Betsey and I slipped and fell, scraping my shin along the stones? Beads of blood sprang to the surface of my skin, followed by a sharp, stinging pain. Mother had dried my tears, her tender kisses helping to soothe the pain.

Where were Fanny and James? Would they come to help me?

Trembling, I held out my left hand, the one I didn't use to write in the sand when I was helping Miss Fanny with her letters.

"Turn your face away. I do not wish to look at you!" commanded Mrs Prudden.

As she brought down the switch, it made a swooshing noise. The instant it hit my palm, I felt a red-hot snap of agony and jerked my hand away. Howling, I cradled my palm to my chest as tears sprang to my eyes.

"How dare you move!" Mrs Prudden shrieked. I dared a sideways glance at her. Could she really mean to strike me again?

Her grey eyes glittered. Her lips were a grim, thin line. She wanted to show me that she was in charge; I understood that now. But how much more pain did she intend to cause?

"I'm so s-sorry, Mrs Prudden," I stammered, still clutching my throbbing hand. Perhaps, if I appealed to her caring, motherly side, she would stop and think about what she was doing to me.

"Give me your hand!" she screamed. I flinched and held my hand out. She did not look at me, she did not pause – and this time she arched her arm up even higher and brought the switch down even harder.

Thwack!

I gasped. I stared at my palm. The skin was split and a line of bright blood swam to the surface. Mrs Prudden and I stared at the blood as it pooled in my cupped palm. I bit my bottom lip hard.

The silence between us felt heavy; my blood dripped onto the floor and only then did she seem to come to her senses. Clearing her throat, she put the switch down on the chair next to her.

"Clean yourself up before you handle the baby," she said. Then she left the room, leaving me stunned and crying.

So, there it was. I suddenly, all in an instant, understood all the furtive looks I had witnessed over the years between people in the Williams household. I now understood the change between my mother and Mrs Williams during those times when Captain Williams returned home. I could now appreciate the raised whispers and excuses made when Mother limped.

This is what it was to grow up – to understand the cruelty people are capable of inflicting on one another. To truly see that my world was based on unfairness. People were not treated equally, even though we all breathed the same air and our hearts pumped the same red blood through our veins. White people had all the power and we had none. I did not know how things had come to be this way, but I could no longer ignore it. Here, in this place and this time, I was worth less than nothing to these people.

That first strike ended my childhood. I withdrew inside myself; my heart closed over and my skin became tougher. I vowed that however often they beat my body, they would never hurt my mind and spirit. There would always be a place inside me that the white people could not reach. And with hope, love and knowledge, my mind and spirit would grow ever stronger.

Along with my new resolve was a world-weary sadness too. I grieved the loss of my true mistress, Mrs Williams, and for the happiness I had known when I lived in her home.

I was a slave. My life was not my own and perhaps it never would be. This harsh fact seeped into my mind and down, down into my bones every day as I hoed the weeds, washed the dishes, chopped vegetables, looked after the baby, helped Miss Fanny with her lessons and scrubbed the stone floors and white walls...

Sometimes, I wondered about the stories I'd heard from people discussing the newspapers in the stores and streets, about the folks across the sea who had escaped to freedom. At night, I would lie awake and gaze up at the moon. Over and over, I would whisper to myself, *"Run ... escape ... freedom!"* I would trace the letters on my arm. Each word was like an arrow – straight and true and able to protect me. I kept them safe and secret, hoping that in the future I would have the chance to use them.

The words *escape* and *freedom* became my daily prayers and companions. I did not let my situation wear me down or make me weak. Instead, I realized how being almost invisible was an advantage; I could soak up everything I heard and saw. When visitors came, no one paid me any attention, so I heard more about news and politics than Fanny and James would have been allowed to hear.

Sometimes, when Fanny, James, baby Daniel and I went to the beach, I felt free – drawing letters in the sand, the seawater lapping my ankles. I listened to birdsong, and with the sun warming my skin and the fragrant scent of purple hibiscus on the breeze, I remembered what a beautiful place the world could be.

I tried to keep my mind on learning and not dwell on how much I missed Mother, Betsey or dear, dear Mrs Williams. Although they lived on in my heart, my heart had been sealed – life was easier that way. Most days, I even managed to smile. At night, in my mind, I sang the songs Mother and I used to sing, and relived the games Betsey and I played, remembering how we wound pink blooms through each other's hair on those sunny, simple days.

A few weeks later, when I was working in the garden, Mrs Prudden appeared. She took the hoe from my hands and leaned it against the fence.

"I have news," she told me.

I scanned her face for signs of annoyance – was another beating coming? But there were none.

"Mary, you are not to work for me any more," she continued.

I felt a pang of despair. How had I displeased her? I worked hard and never complained. My mother would be so disappointed! Before I could ask her why, Mrs Prudden smiled at me.

"You have been a good worker. I will be sorry to see you

go. But you still belong to Mr Williams, and it so happens that your master is getting married again. He intends to sell you and your two sisters to raise money for his wedding."

Reeling, I tried to make sense of her words. My sisters and I were going to be rounded up and sold off to the highest bidder? I could scarcely bear to think about it.

Mrs Prudden turned away. "You may go and get yourself ready."

I sank to my knees, the soft soil clinging to my osnaburg dress. Sobbing, questions thundered through my mind. What would become of me? Who would buy me? Where would I go and what would I do? What kind of future was in store for me?

All these questions weighed heavily on my mind but all I could do was obey my mistress. So I said my goodbyes to Miss Fanny and James and wept when I hugged baby Daniel. I could hardly believe that I would never see them again.

The only good thing was that I would be with my mother and siblings again, even though I knew it would not be for long.

When I arrived at the Williams residence, Betsey rushed out to meet me.

"My dear Molly!" she cried, throwing her arms round me. We squeezed each other tight – as sisters might – and tears of happiness filled my eyes, even though the reason for our meeting was so sad and scary.

"It is so good to see you again!" said Betsey.

"And you too!" I said, meaning every word. "But what is to become of us now?"

"You are my slaves and Father has no right to sell you!" Betsey was furious but we both knew that she would have to obey her father, no matter what her own wishes were.

"Your mother is living nearby with my aunt," explained Betsey. "Let's go there now, it's only a short walk."

Betsey and I walked there in silence, unable to properly enjoy our reunion, knowing that this was our last day together. When we reached the top of the hill and looked down at the house overlooking the ocean, my heart thumped against my ribs. Inside that house, my mother and sisters were waiting for me.

"Let's go and find out what the plans are for tomorrow," Betsey said, taking my hand and squeezing it.

As soon as I walked into the house, my poor mother burst into tears. I had never heard wailing like it, and to this day, the sound of her crying still fills my nightmares.

"My poor babies!"

Mother opened her arms and I rushed into them. She squeezed me so tight that I could barely breathe, and it struck me then, for the first but not the last time, how unfair this world could be. I had never before – nor since – suffered such sorrow as I felt in her arms just then.

"How can God allow this?" I whispered into her ear as she held me close.

"Shush now, child," she soothed, sniffing back her tears, and stroking the hair off my forehead. "The sooner you become used to the ways of this world, the better you will be able to bear them."

But I did not want to hear her being so accepting. She was wise but resigned to her fate, while fire surged in my belly and bile rose in my throat. I wanted to *do* something ... fight or *R-U-N*! I did not want to say goodbye to the people I loved all over again; I did not want to leave them and face the unknown.

That evening, the hours went so slowly it almost felt as if time were going backwards. Even after my long, tiring walk, I could not face any food. In the kitchen, I lay down to sleep, the blankets wrapped tightly around me. But every time I closed my eyes, the sound of Hannah and Dinah's sobbing chilled me to my bones.

In the morning, when I woke, my eyes sore and stinging, it took me a moment to remember where I was.

Today was a sad day indeed! The day I would be sold. It still didn't feel real to me. Who would my new owner be? Where and how would I be set to work?

The mood was gloomy and everyone was silent. Hannah, Dinah and I gave each other small smiles as we struggled into the new osnaburg dresses we'd been given so that we would look respectable at market.

"Taking my own babies to be sold ... what a task for a mother!" said Mother, who looked sadder than I'd ever seen her. As she dabbed at her tears, I vowed not to cry; if I wept too, then Mother would find this day even more unbearable.

She called Betsey in to say goodbye to us. Betsey and I embraced one last time.

"I can't believe that Papa is selling *my* slave!" she cried. "It's breaking my heart to lose you."

I did not have the heart to reply that I did not want to be anyone's slave, but the truth was that I would rather be her slave than be heading to the unknown fate that awaited me.

"Let me take my little chicks to market," Mother said, sighing wearily as she wiped her tears and fixed a little black hat on my head.

Chapter 5

Hamilton, Bermuda
(Hamble Town)

1800

Mother, Hannah, Dinah and I took the road to Hamble Town and reached the market around four in the afternoon. Normally, the market would be an exciting place to visit, but not today.

Mother lined us up, eldest to youngest, against the wall of a big house. I stared at her, my bottom lip wobbling. She nodded, her eyes fixed on me firmly. I felt her pain, saw it in her eyes. She tried her best to stand proud and strong for us, but every time she fixed our hats or flattened our hair, her fingers would quiver.

The three of us stood silently, arms folded and staring straight ahead. Next to me, I felt Hannah's legs trembling; I wanted to reach out my hand to comfort her, but I didn't dare.

A crowd of white folk gathered round us.

"Wonder what they'll go for," said one.

The way their gazes lingered made my skin crawl.

"Strong legs, that one," continued the man, looking me up and down. "Good for lifting bales, I'll bet."

"I'm not sure," said another. "Look at that glint in her eye. She looks as if she's full of her own ideas, and that won't do. There's not a boy or man among 'em!"

Several of the men in the group looked as if they might be cruel owners, with their fat, fleshy faces. They looked at my mother appraisingly.

"This one has borne strong stock," one laughed, smoke from his pipe curling into the air and making my eyes water.

The smell of the smoke made me feel quite sick, but not as sick as their comments. My blood began to boil, anger rushing in to replace the sadness. I balled my fists tightly in my pockets, glad that no one could see them. How dare those men talk about us as if we were no more than cattle!

"Who is he?" I hissed, as a stout white man waddled towards us.

"He is the vendue master – the auctioneer – and you must do as he says," Mother explained.

"What will I have to do?" I asked, suddenly fearful again. I had not had much experience of a male master, but I sensed, by the sweat and stink of these men, their rough hands and crooked smiles, that they would not be kind or fair.

Mother leaned close and lowered her voice. "The vendue master will announce the asking price for each of you, then conduct the sale."

He came over and circled us, staring intently. It was as if his eyes were burning into my soul, splitting it apart. I had always been taught it was rude to stare at others in such a blatant way. But as usual, it was one rule for the white people, especially men, and another for us.

"Who's the eldest?" he barked at my mother, waving his hand dismissively at the three of us.

My mother lowered her eyes and pointed shakily at me.

"Come!" he grabbed my hand, squashing my fingers, and forced me into the middle of the marketplace. "We'll start with you."

The crowd was larger now, and the men watched us carefully as they laughed and jostled one another. The vendue master gripped my shoulders firmly and turned me slowly around.

I felt eyes all over me, sizing me up as if I were a piece of meat. I did not know where to look. If I stared back at them, I would be seen as insolent, so I cast my eyes down to the ground. Tears filled my eyes as I tried to focus on a tiny purple petal, skittering along the ground as it was buffeted by the wind.

Soon, there were hands all over me. I stiffened and half-closed my eyes so I did not have to see their faces close-up. I could hear everything they said about me, but they did not seem to care. They said disgusting things and brayed, laughing, as they squeezed my thighs and calves to see if I had any muscles and examined my upper arms to assess my strength.

How I longed to push away those hands with their dirty fingernails. But I knew that if I did, I would bring shame to my mother and punishment to my sisters as well as me. So I held my breath. I thought of days long ago, when Betsey and I played together as Mother sang to us, and when I sat with Miss Fanny, dangling baby Daniel's toes in the water, hearing his high-pitched giggles as I tickled his tummy.

"Let's start the bidding!" the vendue master shouted, snapping his heels together.

The sound brought me back to the present. I raised my head, blinked back my tears and focused my eyes on a spot on the bark of the tree opposite me.

"Fifteen pounds!" a voice cried.

"Twenty," said another.

Men yelled out different bids and I stood, trembling and

terrified, as the numbers rose higher and higher. Was it good if I fetched a high price? My worth as a human being was based on what a man was willing to pay. I thought to myself that markets should be for selling food, livestock or clothes ... not *people*!

"I'll take her for thirty pounds," called a deep voice.

"She looks strong, let's say forty," yelled another man.

The louder the men became, the more my stomach churned. They weren't bidding for a calf or a lamb – they were discussing me, a human being, a sister, a friend, my mother's *daughter*!

Eventually, the voices and clamour died down. After a brief lull, the vendue master cried:

"Fifty-seven pounds! SOLD to Captain John Ingham!"

The crowd whooped and cheered as if they had witnessed some worthy event. The buyer was congratulated, and people commented that I had fetched a good sum for such a young slave.

Whoever this man was, he would be my third owner.

Then my sisters were led forward, and I watched as both were bid for and sold to different masters. This broke my heart, because I had secretly hoped that we would be sold to the same person. Mother came and put her arms around us. We huddled together.

"My girls, keep a good heart, do your duty and obey your masters."

"When will we see you?" I asked her, tears pricking my eyes and my throat tightening.

She shook her head. "Know that my love and God's love will always be with you."

A rough hand grabbed my arm and yanked me away from my mother.

"Come now!" a voice barked. I turned to see a tall man glaring at me, his lip curling. "Follow me!"

Next to him was a boy about my age. He sneered, narrowing his eyes. "Did you hear your new master?" the boy said. "Follow my father!"

Chapter 6

Pembroke Parish, Spanish Point, Bermuda

1800

I wish I could write that this was a new start, and that hope blossomed on taking up my new position. But the truth is that from that moment, my life became the worst of nightmares.

Even my deepest, darkest fears would not, could not, have prepared me for my new life. As I followed that man, I lost the last of my innocence and childhood, never to be recovered.

"I am Benjy," the boy said, as I fell into step beside him. "My father, Captain John Ingham, owns a store here in Hamilton. He is also a privateersman – a very important citizen!"

"Where do you live?" I asked, careful to keep my eyes on the road ahead of me and my voice low and polite. I glanced sideways and knew that he was sizing me up, wondering what kind of person I was.

"We live at the Ingham farm at Spanish Point," he answered. And then, adopting a haughty tone, he added, "You'll see soon enough. And asking questions of your masters is impertinent."

I knew then that my new owners were not going to be like my previous ones. Betsey and I had been almost like friends, and my only duty was to be her playmate. Even at the Pruddens', I was valued enough to look after baby Daniel and help Miss Fanny with her learning. But I could tell from the sharp set of this boy's jaw and his swaggering walk that here was someone who desperately wanted to follow in his father's footsteps as a master. He needed to prove himself, and I knew I would have to be very careful around him. I sighed to myself, feeling anxious.

As we walked, I tried to focus on the future; I would work hard and make Captain Ingham glad that he had bought me. But I kept recalling my poor mother's weeping, and my sisters' cries were still echoing in my ears.

Darkness had fallen by the time we arrived at Spanish Point, but even so I could see how large the house at the bottom of the hill was.

The captain turned off the path, waving Master Benjy to go on ahead. I followed Benjy, but stopped when I saw two women working in the yard. They raised their faces to look at me, their smiles full of kindness and pity.

"Welcome," said one of the women.

"Poor, poor child," murmured the other. "You are no more than a babe."

I tried to return their smiles, but the women looked so bone-weary and scrawny that I couldn't help shuddering at the thought that soon I might be just like them.

"If you keep God's words in your heart and your mind pure, you might make it through," the first woman muttered, as Benjy roughly shoved me inside the house.

"Go and wait in the corner of that room there. Mother will come and give you your instructions," he said.

I walked nervously into a chilly parlour and stood in the corner. The air itself felt unforgiving. Now that I was alone, I could not stop my tears; they streamed down my cheeks faster than I could wipe them away.

I pressed my lips together to stop my sobs escaping, but I had never felt a sadness as heavy as in that moment. I realized that I was all alone. My future life stretched out ahead of me: long days of lonely, backbreaking work.

"Quit your snivelling!" said a sharp voice.

A tall, stout woman with a swarthy complexion was frowning at me. Her eyebrows were dark and drawn together, her fleshy lips turned down. My tears stopped instantly, and I was seized with fear. This woman had no love or kindness in her heart – I instinctively knew this as surely as I knew the sun went down each evening.

"Here!"

She thrust a fat, wriggling baby into my arms, and I fumbled for a second, trembling with tiredness and unsure of the baby's weight.

"In this house you will not cry. There is no place for tears here, do you understand?" she snarled.

I winced because her voice was full of sharpness and her words wounded me. I nodded, unable to trust myself to speak without starting to cry again.

"You'd better not be a mute." She sighed and squinted at me, muttering, "You'll be looking after the babies and the farm animals, as well as your duties in the house." She snatched at my hat and tossed it across the room. "No need for such fripperies while you're under my roof. Now go to the kitchen and make yourself known."

Then she turned and marched out of the room, leaving me with the baby.

I found my way to the kitchen, which was separate to the main house.

As I bounced the baby on my hip, the kitchen door

burst open. A woman entered, murmuring in a strange tongue I had not heard before.

"Please, what is that language you are speaking?" I asked, curiosity getting the better of me. The words that flowed from her lips sounded like music.

"*Je parle en français*," she said. "I am speaking French."

"It sounds so beautiful," I said.

She smiled at me, but her eyes remained sad. "It *is* beautiful," she said.

She was very tall, and her belly bulged – she was going to have a baby.

"I have come to live here," I said. She looked me up and down and her smile was wide and genuine. My heart sang at this small gesture of kindness.

"Is this your first time as a slave?" she asked, kindly.

I nodded, then shrugged. "This kind of slavery, yes," I replied. I tried not to think of Betsey and our games or of Fanny and her letters and lessons. I could tell that life was going to be very different here. My days of playing and learning were over.

"I'm Hetty," she said. "You will do well here if you work hard. I've already milked the cows and now I must put the sweet potatoes on for supper. Come – if you watch me work, you will learn the ways of the Ingham residence."

I had never seen anyone work so determinedly. I followed Hetty, carrying the baby, as she herded the sheep and put them into their enclosure. Then she drove the cattle home and I watched as she fed and rubbed down Captain Ingham's horse and gave the other animals their supper.

Then we went to the main house, where she walked from room to room, preparing the bedrooms. Then she got the children ready for bed. Once we had tucked the other children in for the night, she took the baby from me and laid it down to sleep too. She performed all these tasks perfectly.

Back in the kitchen, she turned to me and smiled, and I thought my heart would burst at the kindness I sensed within her.

"Come, you must be hungry," she said

I nodded and sat down to a supper of potatoes and milk. While I ate, I listened carefully as she told me the ways of the house.

"This is for you," Hetty said, holding out a thick blanket. I draped it round my shoulders as I finished my supper.

"You will sleep outside Mrs Ingham's room. Whenever she calls out, you must do whatever she asks. Do you understand?"

"I do."

"I do not know where you have come from, or what

45

your previous masters expected," said Hetty. "But you are young, so I will offer this advice. Do not ever talk to, argue with or question them. Do what they tell you immediately and to the best of your ability. Save the talking for when you are with your kind; there are many slaves here on the captain's plantation."

"D-do you like it here?" My voice was a small whisper in the night air.

Hetty gazed at me. She shrugged her thin shoulders. "What is there to like if one is not free?" she asked quietly, lowering her head and looking at the floor.

"Come now. You must rest," she said. "The mistress has a strict schedule and I still have a lot to do."

It wasn't comfortable, lying in the corridor outside the mistress's room. But I was careful not to make too much noise, conscious even of the floorboards underneath me creaking, since the master and mistress had been in bed for hours. But I was so weary that I quickly fell into a deep sleep. Then, suddenly, a sharp voice woke me – Mrs Ingham's.

"And have you not yet finished, girl?"

I sat up, scared. Did she mean me?

Then Hetty's voice came from below.

"No, Mistress, not yet!"

The door to the Inghams' bedroom was flung open and the captain stormed out, dressed in his nightshirt. I gulped as I glimpsed the length of twisted cowskin leather in his hand. He almost kicked me as he passed by and thundered downstairs.

Crack!

I sat bolt upright, clutching the blanket to my chest and winced as I heard the snapping and thwacking sounds coming from below.

Hetty screamed out. "Oh, Massa! Have mercy upon me, Massa!" Her voice cracked as she wailed and begged.

I started shaking uncontrollably. Hetty – lovely, kind, hardworking Hetty – was being beaten! Why, when she had done nothing wrong? What could this mean? Were my sisters experiencing the same fate in other houses across the island? Would the master come for me next? Long after the house fell silent again, I sat, wide awake and afraid. I would never know another night as long as my first under Captain Ingham's roof. I thought the dawn would never come.

Chapter 7

Pembroke Parish, Spanish Point, Bermuda

1800

The next morning, I was sent to cut stalks from the papaya trees on the hillside by the house. I'd been taught to do this at the Pruddens' and was glad to be outdoors, with the sun on my back. Here, I could almost forget the brutality of the night before. I tried to tell myself that maybe it hadn't been so bad – that it was my own fear and sorrow which had made the screams seem louder.

"Hello," said a voice.

I stopped work and turned round. Two boys were grinning at me.

"I'm Cyrus," said the boy with paler skin.

"And I'm Jack," said the other.

As no one was watching us, we spoke for a while. I told

them about being sold at Hamble Town market and they stared at me, wide-eyed.

"You must be very strong to fetch such a sum," Jack said.

I shrugged. "I don't think I'm any stronger than anyone else."

"How long have you worked for the Inghams? Do your parents work here too?" I asked, happy to meet others close to my age. Having companions might make life less lonely.

They both shook their heads. Jack said, "I'm from Guinea, but a sailor sold me to Captain Ingham."

"I've been here since I was a baby," added Cyrus.

I noticed cuts and scars criss-crossing their arms and legs. The memory of the cries from last night made me shiver, despite the heat.

"Molly!"

I was being called. I knew I was not here to talk and make friends, so as fast as I could, I ran straight back up to the house.

Mrs Ingham stared at me, unsmiling. "I will instruct you in your tasks, and I will show you once only. I hope you are as strong as you look and can follow basic instructions. Pay attention or you will feel a whip against your skin."

"Yes, Mistress," I said.

"From April to August you will pick cotton," she told me.

"You need to carefully tend the plants and weed the cotton rows in the fields. Inside, your duties are to clean the house, wash the floors and help with the cooking and baking. These will be your main duties but we may call upon you to do other things."

Mrs Ingham showed me around the house and grounds and explained everything that she expected of me. There was such a lot to remember that my head felt heavy with the weight of her words.

But no matter how different life is from what one has known before, we humans are amazing in our ability to adjust and become used to new routines. The days and weeks passed, and we worked from sunrise to sunset. There was no time to be sad or to dream of a different life. Whenever I wasn't working or resting my aching body, I would recite the letters and words I'd learned with Fanny to keep my mind active.

I took to calling Hetty 'Aunty' and she smiled at this. We worked together well.

But one night, something terrible happened. Even though the cow had been tied up the night before, somehow it got loose and escaped. Both Jack and Cyrus were frightened that they might be blamed.

I was in the kitchen when Jack hurried in, panting.

"Oh, Mary! The Captain – he's beating Hetty something awful!" he cried.

"Can't we do anything?" I asked.

Jack shook his head and wiped away a tear. "There's nothing any of us can do." He slumped into a chair, hopeless. "It's as if he has a devil inside him when this mood takes hold of him."

Then Cyrus rushed in. "Stay out of the yard if you know what's good for you," he said to me, frantically. "Poor Hetty, she's … she's being tied to a tree!"

Tied to a tree? I tried to make sense of what Cyrus was saying. A beating was harsh enough, but what sort of punishment was this?

"Come!" Cyrus pulled Jack to his feet. "The master says we have to hold Hetty still, or it will be us next!"

I gripped the table as the boys shuffled into the yard. I trembled – surely the master would not call me out too? As I scraped the potatoes I hummed to myself, but I couldn't block out Hetty's shattering screams.

"There must be a life better than this!" I told myself as I scrubbed, my palms becoming red and raw from the bristles. I wept for Hetty and her unborn child. What a world this was! How cruel and unfair that we should have to endure all this agony and daily humiliation!

I am thankful that I didn't see Cyrus and Jack carry Hetty, battered and bruised, back into the kitchen. Later, they told me that she had been taken to an outbuilding. While Hetty was recovering from her injuries, all her tasks fell to me. I was busy from dawn until the dead of night, but I was glad to have work to prevent me from thinking too much. Being bone-tired at the end of the day stopped the dark, dismal thoughts which pulled at my mind and threatened to drag me under. I refused to let myself go to such a hopeless place. I clung to the idea that one day – one precious day – I would *R-U-N*!

As soon as I could, I sneaked in to see Hetty, careful to ensure the master didn't see me. I was afraid that if he did, I might suffer the same fate as my beloved Aunty.

"Hetty!" I cried, my heart breaking to see her lying there, so still and bruised.

She took my hand in hers, and it saddened me to see her so weak, her grip so feeble. She tried to smile but her lips cracked as she did so.

"My child," she murmured, "I hope … I hope that one day you will be far from here. *Je prie pour toi.* I pray for you."

I bit my lip, hoping the same thing. *R-U-N!* I thought to myself, quickly trying to dismiss the idea. Yet "*R-U-N*" stayed in my head all day; a song, a chant, a command – echoing with every step I took.

Life went on. Almost daily, I was on the receiving end of Mrs Ingham's brutality. She enjoyed robbing me of my sleep, making me wash clothes and dishes late into the night, and endlessly picking cotton or shearing wool throughout the day. She may not have been as strong as her husband, but she did not hold back when she flogged me with her cowskin, a strap made from leather.

Every morning before the sun came up, I milked the Inghams' eleven cows. I didn't mind this task, even though the weeds, full of dew, tickled my bare calves. I would wrap my hands round the cows' warm teats, squeezing and pulling as I'd been shown. The scent of the fresh milk as it streamed into the bucket was sweet and soothing. The cows were mostly placid and, as the sun rose, birdsong filled the air. I enjoyed the peace of these early mornings before my mind become crowded with all the tasks I had to remember to do.

Sadly, poor Hetty died. I had hoped that she was getting better – I prayed every night for her– but this is not a fairy story and my friend just could not recover from the master's merciless beating.

Knowing that I lived under the roof of such a ruthless man, I cried myself to sleep each night. I moved through the days as if I too were dead – my bones aching and heavy, my heart dull and empty. There was no hope and no happiness in my life. I longed for those days when Betsey would comb out my hair, or make me put on silly voices for her dolls. And I longed for the evenings too, when I would sit at Mother's feet and listen to her sing.

Hetty's death changed Jack and Cyrus, too. Their smiles and easy laughter disappeared, and they stuck to one another like glue as they tended the grounds and gardens. I sometimes watched them hoeing and weeding, but we barely had the chance to exchange words. The sharp eyes of Mrs Ingham were always on us, and even a small smile was not worth the pinching and poking that she seemed to enjoy as she passed us by.

One day, the weather was particularly squally; rain and wind lashed against the house.

"Mary!" Mrs Ingham roared. "Go out and empty that earthenware pot!"

Outside, I braced myself against the wind and rain and stared at the big pot in dismay – it had a huge crack running the length of it. And as I tipped it to empty the water, the whole pot split in two!

I ran inside. "I'm sorry, Mistress, but the pot has broken," I said.

Mrs Ingham set aside her sewing, her teeth gritted. "You broke it!"

I shook my head. "No, no! It was already cracked…"

"You imbecile!" She did not want to hear any words from me. I knew that she was angry because of the rain and the tasks she could not do outside. I had managed three days with no beatings, but I knew I wouldn't escape one that day.

"Come directly to me," she ordered, her voice icier than the wind tearing through the trees.

She lifted my osnaburg dress and whipped her cowskin across my back. Each time she paused, I prayed that my punishment was over, but something unholy possessed her that day. She was the one howling with each fresh lash she delivered; I bit my lip, staying silent, trying to fill my mind with thoughts of flowers and sweet milk and molasses, bananas and bluebirds. As she continued, I silently recited prayers I had heard from other slaves.

When Captain Ingham came home, his wife told him of my behaviour and the broken pot. He decided that I had not received enough punishment, and that he too would teach me a lesson.

Swearing, he set upon me, beating his fists against my body. All the while, I steeled myself not to cry out. As his blows rained down upon my head and my back, I took my mind and my pain, my shame and my sorrow, across to the other side of the island, to the sea and the ships.

"You do not even cry!" bellowed the captain. "Well, tomorrow, I will lash you a hundred times. You can be sure of that!"

That night I hardly slept. All I could think of was the lashes that were coming in the morning. I knew that Captain Ingham was a man of his word.

When dawn broke, the captain hauled me outside and along the ground by the collar of my dress. Then he tied my hands to a ladder in the barn so that I could not move. Cruel, wicked man! What kind of person could commit such atrocities against another human being? Why did the law only protect some people and not all of them?

"Benjy, keep count!" he instructed his son, who was standing to the side.

"One!" Benjy counted aloud, steady and sure. How proud he was to help his father!

Captain Ingham lashed my skin again and again. I lifted my face upward and listened to the wind and the rain batter the house. There was no sunshine that day, no warmth to be found anywhere.

After a while, Benjy began to look concerned. "Father, rest a while," he suggested. "You have gone quite pale."

Ingham slumped into a chair. "Fetch me something to drink," he growled at his son.

If my wrists had not been bound to the ladder, I too would have collapsed. I could feel wet, slick blood streaming down my body, but my cheeks were bone dry – my pain was too intense for tears.

The air inside the barn felt thick, sticky and stifling. Benjy and Mrs Ingham both rushed in. Mrs Ingham fussed over her husband while Benjy paced back and forth.

"Oh, you have exerted yourself too much!" she scolded, fussing round her husband as he flopped back, tired and lifeless.

Serves you right! The thought pounded like a drum through my mind. What if he died right here and now?

CRASH!

An almighty clatter came from above – some of the roof timbers had collapsed, just above the captain's chair. Leaping out of the way, he stared up in dismay.

"What the…?" he stammered.

"The Lord is punishing us," shrieked Mrs Ingham, glaring at me. "Have mercy upon us!"

My mind swam with thoughts I could never dare to say, but I hoped no mercy would be granted to these people – people who, with all their wealth and privilege, did not have the decency to treat their workers with mercy or compassion.

"Quiet woman, it's an earthquake!" exclaimed the captain. "Can't you feel the ground beneath us shuddering?"

I closed my eyes and held my breath. It was as if the good Lord had picked up the island and tipped it upside down before giving it a good shake. I imagined that He was shaking Bermuda to rid it of those people who treated their fellow humans so cruelly. I slumped in my restraints, my whole body sore and exhausted, as the ground groaned and shook beneath me.

Maybe this was how my life would end? If death was coming, I did not much care. Perhaps the next life would treat me more kindly than this one. My eyelids fluttered and shut as I imagined clouds, as soft as the cotton I picked from the fields, lifting me up and carrying me away...

Chapter 8

Pembroke Parish, Spanish Point, Bermuda

1801

The earthquake caused much damage on the island, and to the Inghams' property, but the captain didn't die and nor did I, although it took me weeks to recover from my cruel beating.

When you are beaten regularly, after a while it is not the kicks and blows themselves that are the worst things to bear, but the uncertainty – the feeling that you never know when the next beating is coming.

My master and mistress were impossible to please – I soon learned that that there seemed no rhyme nor reason to their fits of rage. I could never tell what might set off their attacks on me. The fear never left me, and I would shudder and flinch whenever either of them walked past me as I did my chores.

I felt myself shrinking with each day that passed. I stooped and bowed my head; my future plans and ideals were all but wiped away.

Some time after the earthquake, I was in the yard milking a cow when another cow trotted past and started munching the sweet potato seedlings. I tried to shoo the animal away, but it was far too hungry.

Captain Ingham was nearby and when he saw what was happening, he took off one of his heavy boots and hurled it at me. I tried to dodge it, but the boot hit me in the small of my back. My shrieks startled the cow I'd been milking, and she kicked over the pail of milk I'd collected.

Seeing the wasted milk pooling on the ground made the captain even angrier! But if he hadn't thrown his boot, the cow would not have been startled. Captain Ingham was always making situations worse by losing his temper suddenly, then blaming everyone and everything around him.

Sometimes, when I lay on the cold floor outside my mistress's room, clutching my blanket, trying to keep warm, I could scarcely get comfortable due to all my cuts and bruises. Sleep escaped me; I could never relax enough to rest because I knew that, at any moment, I could be summoned to do her bidding.

One night as I lay there, tired and sore, a familiar word appeared, as if it had been written on the inside of my skull, behind my eyes.

RUN!

I tossed and turned, but the thought would not leave me be. The words *Run, run, run!* took on a life of their own, dancing behind my eyes. Every time I tried to think of something else – what I might cook the next day or some words Jack had said to me – the words just came back into my mind, stronger than ever.

RUN!

I shivered – whether from the cold, or from the daring plan planting itself in my mind, I could not tell. But I started to take the thought seriously. Oh, to see Mother again! I knew that she now lived at Mr Darrell's residence in Cavendish. She might be displeased with me for running away, but anything had to be better than my life here. What the master and mistress demanded of me was so unfair! I worked from sunrise to past sunset. I never complained or disobeyed them. I tried my best always, but it made no difference. They seemed to enjoy physically abusing me at every opportunity, never offering me even the smallest crumb of kindness.

Outside, it was cool and quiet. A huge, round moon hung

in the sky, lighting my path. I smiled for the first time in weeks, feeling that the earth was showing its support for my decision to leave. I would visit my mother, and nothing would stop me. I knew I would have to be careful and stick close to the bushes that lined the path; I did not want anyone to see me and drag me back.

I hummed as I walked, focusing on putting one foot in front of the other. Sometimes, in my fear, I thought I could hear horses' hooves behind me, but it was just the wind.

When my throat became dry, I stopped humming and turned to thinking instead. I felt sorry that I had been driven to abandon my post, but the further I got from the Ingham residence, the lighter my heart became. I breathed in the sea air and imagined what it would be like to be free. It would be so sweet! I tried to think of what I would do with my life, if I could choose. I had heard that slaves were being freed in other parts of the world. Would freedom ever be granted to us here in Bermuda?

I sneaked into Mr Darrell's kitchen, softly stepping over the slaves asleep on the floor. I looked round the still, silent room, and there, with a young one nestled on either side of her, was my mother. I nearly yelled out, I was so overjoyed to see her gentle face. I stared at her for what felt like an age, warmth flooding through my heart, barely noticing my tired, throbbing feet.

I leaned over and grasped her hand. I traced her fingers, calloused by hard work, with my thumb. She stirred and startled a little. As she opened her eyes she murmured, "Oh what a dream, that my Mary returns to me once again."

"It's not a dream, Mother – I'm really here," I whispered.

"Child!" she squealed, sitting upright. Then she swiftly covered her mouth with her other hand and put a finger to her lips. "Shh, do not speak." She stood, still clutching my hand, and led me outside.

"What are you doing?" Mother whispered. "The moment your master knows you are missing, he will come for you!" I'd never seen her eyes so wide and scared.

I told her of all I'd been through. My heart ached to see her face droop and her tears fall.

"I hoped … I hoped you would be bought by kinder people," she said. "But so many masters have no time for goodness and decency. Not when there is cotton to be picked and money to be made. Not when these people believe that we are unworthy of even the most basic rights."

We cried and hugged each other close. I drank in her scent, her strong arms holding me tight. I knew then that I would never let anyone break my spirit – not when I had my mother to think of.

She held me in her arms as if I were a baby again and reassured me there was hope for us. She told me she had heard about an enslaved woman called Elizabeth Freeman in a place called Massachusetts in America, who had shown great determination and grit. Elizabeth brought a lawsuit against her master, John Ashley – and won her freedom! This was the first time I had ever heard of an enslaved person becoming free. So it was possible! How could I give up now?

I knew – I knew! – what a gift life was. The Lord had granted me my life and I could not let it be taken away. I would stand and fight. I would not give in to despair. Hope was out there in the world – I just had to find it. Slaves were fighting back and claiming their freedom ... and I knew now that I had to play my part in this fight against injustice.

"Now you listen, child. Come with me," said my mother. "We'll find you somewhere to stay. God only knows what will become of us, but one thing I know is that I will not send you back to those monsters."

We walked for a while until we reached some rocks by a bay. Mother found an opening that led to a cave.

"You can hide in here," she said. "I'll bring you blankets and food later, when I know that it's safe."

As Mother turned to leave, I began to weep, clinging to her as if I never wanted to let her go. She kissed my face and promised me that she would be back very soon.

After she left, thoughts of her loving words stopped me from being scared, alone in the damp darkness. Soon, I was so overcome with exhaustion that I curled up into a ball and fell fast asleep.

For a few days, life carried on like this; Mother brought me food every night and worried about what would become of me. Full of childish hope, I made grand plans to escape by stowing away on a ship. My bruises faded and my cuts healed over, although my back would always be stiff from when the captain had hit it with his boot.

Mother spoke honestly about the different slave owners she had known and told me some of the terrible things she'd seen and heard. But she offered me hopeful tales too, of slaves who had been set free or who had escaped. She had learned this from overhearing men discussing reports in the newspapers.

I began to think that perhaps one day my life would change. I was young and strong. I just needed to bend like the willow, but not break. Mother explained that strength and will would be our saviours.

She reminded me to strengthen my mind, to go to places deep inside myself that no amount of beating and pummelling could reach.

"Parts of you exist that will always be only yours," she said as she stroked my hair. Her eyes clouded. How much must she have endured over the years? What horrors hadn't she shared, couldn't bring herself to speak of? She had seen just how ugly and corrupt her fellow humans could be, and my heart shrivelled to think of her suffering.

Chapter 9

Devonshire Parish, Cavendish, Bermuda

1801

One evening, just after Mother had left, I heard footsteps crunching over leaves and stones at the entrance to my cave. I froze, clutching my blanket to my chest.

"Mary?"

I gasped when I recognized the voice.

"Father!" I cried happily. I stumbled to meet him and threw my arms around him. I breathed him in, the smell of straw, wood chips and something darker. But he unpeeled my arms from his waist and knelt, looking directly into my eyes. He gently took my upper arms and held me tight.

"Now you listen to me, child, and you listen good," he said, his voice firm, but kind. "I heard that you was here and I know what your mother is doing for you, but she is risking her life every moment that you hide away in here, you understand?"

I nodded, feeling ashamed for the first time.

"Mary, how you conduct yourself reflects on me and your mother too." He sounded old as he continued. "You need to show your master that he got what he paid for. Prove that you won't cause no trouble."

Fury surged inside me then. Why wouldn't my father protect me?

"I can't go back there, Father!" I protested. "Look at what they do to me – *look*!" I lifted my osnaburg and turned round, showing Father the deep scars across my back. Tears ran down my cheeks as I heard my father gasp in horror.

"I'm sorry that you have had to endure such cruelty," my father said, his soft voice like a wave lapping at my ankles. "And you're just a child too. This is not a world any of us would wish on anyone we love and yet it is the world we find ourselves in. But the white man has the upper hand. If you can, you need to bear it. There will come a day when we will be free, and I want you to witness such a time. But oh, Mary! If he finds you…"

My father shook his head, unable to think of the right words. Finally, he said, "Come with me. I'll take you back and try to appeal to the man myself. We'll see what else can be done."

At this, I burst into tears. "Nothing can be done! The man is unholy!"

"Never let anyone hear you speak in this manner!" he said, sternly. "Listen to me. I hope beyond all hope that one day you will be able to earn your own money. There may even come a day when you can buy your own freedom. Have hope, child! Life can change!"

I looked at his tired, brown eyes and scarred arms. Did he really believe life could change? Had I made his life even worse?

I clung to my father's hand as we walked along the road back to the Ingham residence. The sun shone high in the sky and birdsong filled the air.

When we arrived in the yard, Captain Ingham had his back to us, instructing Jack and Cyrus. My father cleared his throat.

"Sir?"

Captain Ingham turned to face us. When he saw me, his face flushed red. He raised his arm, but my father dropped to his knees, wringing his hands.

"Please, sir!" he cried. "I regret that my child ran away from your care. She is here now and will never disrespect you again." The captain marched towards us and scowled at me. My cheeks flushed as I felt heat flooding into them. My father took my hand and squeezed it.

"The treatment she has received has been enough to break her heart. The sight of her wounds has almost broken mine. I implore you, please – be a kinder master in future!"

I waited for the captain to roar with anger as I had heard him so often before. Who was my father, a slave, to dare speak of these matters to a master? Did he not know his place? Wasn't he terrified of punishment? I looked up and saw Mrs Ingham peering down from an upstairs window. The captain glared at my father as if he was about to strike him dead, his eyes full of shock and pure hatred.

Sneering, he said, "The wretch should rightly be flogged for running away!"

But the way my father stared directly into the captain's eyes, not flinching or looking down, seemed to affect the captain. Perhaps he felt remorse for the first time. Perhaps my father, appealing to another father on behalf of a daughter, had finally got through to the captain's sense of decency.

My father's gaze was steady, and eventually, after the longest time, the captain cleared his throat and turned away. "She is treated as she deserves," he said.

I could bear it no longer. I ran to face him, and with my hands squeezed into fists at my side I said, "I shall stand your floggings no longer!"

Captain Ingham bent down and put his face right up to mine. Spittle flew from his lips as he yelled and thundered, but I closed my heart and mind to his words and allowed him to shout himself hoarse.

He reminded me that I was his property, that I was insolent, ungrateful and disobedient. I'd heard speeches like this a hundred times or more. With my father behind me, I stood my ground and answered him.

"I am weary of my life."

"Hold your tongue and go about your work now, girl, or I will find a way to settle you," he snapped.

He sounded as unyielding as ever, but I had seen a flicker of something I hadn't seen before – a spark of fear. That was enough to give me strength.

The captain dismissed Father, and after another sad farewell, he was once again gone from my life. Captain Ingham didn't flog me, and for that I was grateful. I got busy in the kitchen, stoking the cooking pot over the fire.

Chapter 10

Pembroke Parish, Bermuda and Grand Turk Island, Turks and Caicos Islands

1801–1803

I remained in the captain's service for the next three years. My longing for freedom never left me, but as the years wore on, there seemed to be little I could do. For much of the time, the days all passed in much the same way. I did not have time to dream of a different, better life; I simply existed, from one day to the next. But as the time passed, I was becoming older and wiser. I carried more scars inside and outside – and some wounds that would never heal.

One day, Captain Ingham called me to him. "I have sold you," he said abruptly. "I am sending you away on a sloop. You will leave tomorrow."

"Will I be able to…?"

"There will be no time for goodbyes," he interrupted. "Make sure you work hard and show my family name in a good light. I have told them you are strong. Make sure to make me a man of my word."

Much as I was relieved to be free of the captain and his wife, I couldn't help worrying who my new owners might be and what they would be like. Would they treat me fairly or work me to exhaustion? Would they be even worse than the Inghams? Only time would tell.

I discovered that I was being sent to work in the salt ponds on Grand Turk Island with other slaves. These shallow ponds were full of seawater; when the sun evaporated the water, crystals of salt were left behind, ready to be harvested, sold and sent to other countries.

I had never been on a sloop, or any kind of boat, before. I liked the way it bobbed up and down on the surface of the waves. The way that, when the sun was high and clear, the water around us shimmered and sparkled. But on the voyage I became sick and weak, like many of the other slaves – there was not enough food or water for all of us.

As the sloop bobbed along, a kind-looking Black man and woman quietly introduced themselves. "My name is Anthony, and this is my wife, Elizabeth," the man said.

"How much longer until we get there?" I asked.

"I don't know," he replied.

They were a nice couple who shared their food with me, and I was grateful to have them as company.

As I lay on the deck, the huge, white sails shuddering and slapping back and forth in the breeze, I tried to imagine what this next phase of my life might bring.

I overheard some men saying that the distance from Bermuda was eight hundred and fifty miles. They said that the journey could take as little as a week if the winds were favourable. We had been at sea for three weeks already, so those winds were definitely not blowing in our favour!

Anthony told me that there were around forty white families and over twelve hundred slaves on the island. In 1800, a number of slaves had escaped to Haiti, and since then, the masters had brought in tight controls to make sure the same thing didn't happen again.

To escape was a dream every one of us slaves shared. All we talked about was what we would do if and when we were free. We agreed that to be free would be the sweetest thing!

Our food and water ran very low and more than once I thought that it would be the end for me. I wasn't sure how much more I could bear. When I lay down to sleep, I didn't know if my eyes would open in the morning.

After four weeks at sea, we finally arrived. We went ashore at the Grand Quay, and the captain of the ship sent me directly to the house of my new master, another Mr Darrell, though unrelated to the previous Captain Darrell. As I walked through the small town, I marvelled at how different the low, wooden houses looked compared to the grand, white stone houses of the parish I had just left. I remembered that Anthony had told me the whole island was only six miles long.

As I approached the house, I felt my stomach fluttering. Even though I was glad to have left Captain Ingham, I had no idea what to expect – all I could do was hope that I had been sold to kindly people who would treat me fairly. If things didn't go well, there would be no possibility of me running off to my mother or father this time. Whatever came next, I would have to bear alone.

A man stepped towards me, and my heart sank. He was stout and red-cheeked, with a sulky, sour look on his face. I did my best to smile.

"I am here from Captain Ingham," I said politely, and bowed my head a little.

"You will call me Master Darrell. Come with me. I'll show you the salt ponds and you will get to work immediately. The others will explain your duties."

Was he not going to offer me food or allow me to rest after my voyage?

"First, I will show you where you are to sleep. Come!"

I followed him to a long shed which was divided into narrow stalls. There were no mats or blankets, only boards nailed into the ground – I would be expected to sleep here, as if I were a cow or horse.

"Now, to work!" he said.

Up to then, I'd never heard of salt ponds. The land around here was full of shallow hollows, which were set back from the sea. When the tide came in, these dips filled as seawater bubbled up from beneath and between the rocks. These were perfect spaces for making salt. The workers made walls from rocks to create a series of ponds.

When we reached the ponds, I was handed a half-barrel and a shovel. I stood in the briny water, which came up to my knees.

Next to me was an older woman who reminded me a little of my mother. She turned to me and said, "Prepare yourself. The days are long."

"What do we have to do?" I asked, staring around me. Everyone had their heads down.

The woman moved closer to me. "We start our day at

four in the morning, and work in these ponds till nine."

"What about breakfast? They can't expect us to work with no food in our bellies!"

"Shh!" she glanced around nervously, making sure none of the overseers were listening to us. "Breakfast? Boiled corn, and don't you dare linger – you got no time to chew – we gets hurried back here soon as."

"Why such a rush?" I asked.

"Gotta get back to it before the rain comes. If the rain comes, it washes away the salt. Then you'll see the master in a terrible state of agitation."

"I suppose the rain makes him think about the money he's losing."

She nodded gravely. I stuck close to her when we worked.

In the mornings, it became harder to work as the heat from the sun overhead grew stronger. Within days, I developed boils and blisters on my calves and feet from standing in the salt water for hours a day. At night, they would throb, the pain making it almost impossible for me to get comfortable enough to sleep.

"Time!" an overseer called at noon. We downed our buckets and shovels and trudged to the place where we had corn soup for our midday meal. Then it was back to the ponds until dusk.

I raked the salt into huge, white heaps, then carried it over to the big deposits and bagged it up for shipping. And then we went down to the harbour, where I washed my skin and cleaned the salt from my barrows and shovels. Finally, we loaded the salt onto the ships that were anchored there.

Then, and only then, could we slowly make our way back up to the house, where our master would give us our allowance of Indian corn. We had to pound it in a mortar before boiling it in water for our supper.

These were long, long days. But even after we had worked a full day, we were not always allowed to stop. Sometimes we worked all night too – turning machines that sucked water out of the sea into the ponds, and measuring out salt to load onto the ships.

The only good thing about this time was that I made my first true friend. One day, I mused aloud that the master seemed very calm. The woman next to me howled with a laugh so deep and rich that it startled me for a moment.

"Why are you laughing?" I asked, smiling myself because her laugh was so infectious.

She wiped at her eyes before appraising me. "Oh, it's not really that amusing," she murmured, her chest still heaving. "It's just that … you're new. Don't mistake the master's quietness for calm. He has a violent, wicked temper but he just don't show it in the same way as some others."

The woman's name was Harriet. I replied that I thought a quiet, angry man might be preferable to a red-faced, screaming one, remembering what I had endured at the hands of the Ingrams. But I could understand what Harriet meant. The matter-of-fact way Master Darrell doled out even the cruellest punishments, as if he were just carrying out an everyday task, was chilling to see.

"Why is this salt so precious?" I asked Harriet. I could understand why people across the sea wanted cotton, sugar and tobacco, but *salt*?

"Salt keeps meat and fish fresh," Harriet said, wiping her hand across her forehead, which was glistening with sweat. "They trade it to many places now; it fetches a good price from countries that can't make their own."

Chapter 11

Grand Turk Island

1803–1813

One exhausting day, the boils on my feet were so bad that I could barely steer my wheelbarrow through the sand.

"Move faster, girl!" Master Darrell hollered.

I tried, I really did, but I stumbled at every step. That night, I lay on the floor of the shed where we slept and whispered to Harriet, "How can you bear it?"

In my years as a slave, I had learned never to complain. I tried always to keep hope in my heart, but that night, with weeping blisters and aching legs, the pain was unbearable. I knew that if I had no sleep, I wouldn't be fit for work in the morning. Then the master would holler even more at me.

"Shush now," said Harriet soothingly. Then she started to sing tenderly under her breath.

"Come, thou Fount of every blessing, tune my
heart to sing Thy grace;
Streams of mercy, never ceasing, call for songs of
loudest praise."

I think the gift of song sustained Harriet and all of us through our long nights of suffering. Lifting up her voice to the Lord gave her a sense of purpose, and a meaning to her life.

"That is such a comforting sound," I said, closing my eyes and letting her voice ease my discomfort.

"The Moravians taught it to me," whispered Harriet. "I went to their church many years ago, when I had a different master, a different life. Those were good people."

I asked her to tell me about her church, and the more she told me, the more determined I was to find myself a Moravian church someday.

"It's Sunday tomorrow," Harriet said quietly. "I will take you into the bush where there is long, soft grass. We can cut it and make mats. When the salt boils are hurting, you can lay them under your legs to protect them from the hard, bare boards."

Over the ten years I worked those salt ponds, my dreams were filled nightly with rocks and salt, sand and sea, shovels and the screams and sighs of slaves. I had never worked so hard in my life. I tried to keep my heart light and my mind nimble – I learned the writing on any packaging that came my way, and at night, Harriet, who had been educated by her previous masters, recited passages to me. She also told me of the many slave revolts across the Caribbean that she had heard of. *"People are fighting back!"* she whispered to me.

During the days, I continued to practise tracing letters in the salt. But life was hard, so hard – a never-ending, living hell. Every day was the same – just endless sea and salt.

Sometimes, as I stood in the water, the salt stinging my cuts and blisters, the sun beating down on my head, sweat trickling down my osnaburg and mingling with the salt, I would think about my mother. Why had she ever brought me into this world? Then I would wonder if my life might have been better if I hadn't enjoyed so much "freedom" in the first twelve years of my life. Those years of being allowed to run around with Betsey gave me the wrong ideas – they made me think that perhaps being owned wasn't so terrible. I could explore Betsey's house and grounds as if they were mine to enjoy. But I knew now that being so free early on only made these later years harder to bear.

Now that I was older, I also began to think about why my mother had so many of us children. I put my hands on my own stomach and wondered what it would be like to grow a life inside me.

How was it for my poor mother to be without her babies and husband day after day, night after night? She'd done no wrong either … yet she was being punished over and over anyhow.

What was the purpose of our time here on this Earth? Surely it was to be of service to the Lord and to be kind to others, but I didn't see any kindness in the masters who had bought me.

No wonder I took pleasure in watching the birds that circled overhead as we worked. Oh, to have wings! Sometimes I'd dream that a gigantic pair of jet-black wings with iridescent feathers had sprung from my back. I would flap them and they would carry me up, high into the sky…

A human being needs to be free.

I do not know what people think of a slave's life, but it is not one of dignity. It is a life of endless toil – even cattle are treated with more compassion! We are worked and flogged so hard that we do not have the strength to think for ourselves, far less to rise up to revolt against our masters. Whole generations of people are worn down, weakened by being overworked and undernourished, disrespected and uncared for. You might make a friend, but just a few days or weeks later, your friend could be sold, or you could find them sick – or dead.

The saddest day of my life came when I met my mother again.

We were on the beach one morning when Harriet shouted, "There's a sloop come in!"

The boat was loaded with a new crop of slaves being brought here to work. When we went aboard to see if we could help, I found my mother was one of the group.

"Mother?" I asked, touching her arm gently. A little girl of around four years old, who she called Rebecca, clung to her, staring at me with big wide eyes.

My mother looked up at me, and I knew, seeing the wild confusion in her eyes, that she did not recognize me. She barely knew where she was. Her mind had gone.

Another slave came to me and gently told me, "We had a terrible storm while on the boat. She didn't react well."

I wasn't surprised. My mother was not used to being at sea, and I remembered how rough my own crossing had been.

"Will she be all right?" I asked, battling back sobs at seeing her in this way.

The man smiled. "I think so. It may take a few days for her to be herself again, but I'm sure she will be well."

She stayed with us for the next week or so and she began to recover a little. But she also had very sad news to share with me – my father had passed away. And she was not even sure where all my other brothers and sisters were now, as they were scattered across different estates. I wondered if we would all ever meet again.

Mr Darrell's son, Dickey, was as heartless as his father. He would stand and watch us work while sneering and jeering.

"I am the overseer!" he would scream. "Me, Master Dickey, and you will respect me!"

We all hated him, and whereas Mr Darrell did not care what we thought of him (in fact, I think he thought us slaves not even capable of thought), Master Dickey yearned for our respect. And although we obeyed him, it was clear to Master Dickey that he commanded no respect from us at all.

"Faster with that barrow!" he would yell, before shoving one of us into the prickly-pear bushes.

When it wasn't salt season, we worked just as hard, building stone walls. We would splash around, spluttering underwater to find the biggest rocks. Then we would hack down the red mangroves and set them ablaze to heat up the seashells we collected. The shells would turn to quicklime and, after water was added, to lime putty, which we used to hold the stones together.

Often, I would stand in the sea, a huge rock in my arms, thinking about what I would like to do with it. Harriet would nudge me, aware of the dark thoughts running through my mind. All of us had the same unspoken thoughts – and who could blame us for wanting to hurl those rocks at our masters?

Then one day, as suddenly as another new routine had begun, it was over. Master Darrell told me I was to go with him to his new home back in Bermuda, where I would wait on his daughters.

Although this was wonderful news, there was also sadness.

"I will be so sorry not to see you again, Harriet," I said, my throat closing up with the tears I was holding back. We embraced each other and squeezed tight.

"You have been a kind and true friend," I whispered.

She smiled sadly. "I will miss your spirit and optimism," she said. "But perhaps our paths will cross again one day. In this life, or the next."

I was sad to leave my fellow slaves behind, but this was a chance to return to my birthplace. I couldn't wait to set foot on home soil again.

Chapter 12

Bermuda and Antigua

1813–1826

What a joy to be back working on Bermudian land! To be planting and hoeing sweet potatoes, cabbages, pumpkins and onions. Picking bananas. Feeling stronger as the boils and blisters from all those years on Grand Turk Island began to heal. Compared to standing in salt water all day long, my new duties of gardening, keeping the house tidy, milking the cows and grooming the horses seemed easy!

I heard from other slaves that in August, a hurricane had hit Grand Turk Island. I thought immediately of my friend Harriet whom I'd left behind.

"What happened?" I asked the man next to me.

He chuckled. I was surprised to see him laugh over such a tragedy.

"Them white men! They never learn – they cannot

mess with God's will. They shoulda known better, not bin so greedy."

"What do you mean?"

"Slaves wanted to build a church. They were willing to lay the stones themselves, but the white men forbade it. Forbade our fellow men from giving thanks to the Lord. Them slaves wanted to give thanks even though they ain't got no occasion to be thankful. And them white men said no."

He wheezed with laughter once more. "Seems only fair that the Lord should be angry and send that wind and rain to wash away their houses!"

I knew it was not proper to think of revenge, but that evening I hoped with all my heart that Master Darrell's and Dickey's houses had been among those swept away. How wonderful if their piles of salt were all ruined, and they went out of business.

I knew my good feeling would not last, and sure enough, I was right. One morning, as I was scrubbing the stone steps, screams came from above. It was Miss Darrell, the master's daughter!

I ran up those stairs as fast as I could. Throwing open the bedroom door, I saw Master Darrell beating his own daughter! She was cowering in a corner, petrified. This man was not only cruel to the people he enslaved – obviously nobody was safe from him! I could not stand by and witness such brutality and, thinking nothing of my own safety, tried to get in between them so that his blows would not reach her. I managed to drag her away and out of the room. Mr Darrell paused, and I hoped that he had come to his senses. But instead, he just turned on me instead! Afterwards, Mr Darrell's daughter thanked me for my bravery, but I had only done what any decent person would do.

Sadly, after witnessing further instances of his brutality, I ran to a nearby house and banged on the door, hoping that a sensible person would answer and hear what I had to say.

"I cannot stay there a moment longer!" I wept to the mistress of the house.

She took pity on me and offered me a hot drink. "If you're a good worker, he can hire you out," she kindly suggested.

Perhaps she spoke to Mr Darrell, or the word got around that I had fled and spoken ill of him, because shortly after I returned, he ordered me to go to Cedar Hill and work there, washing laundry.

I was relieved to be hired out. It was good to be among other women again; as I stood and scrubbed, I felt content to listen and enjoy their conversation.

"Have you heard? Mr Wood is heading off to Antigua!"

I became lost in their beautiful descriptions of Antigua. It sounded heavenly. I had hoped, on my return to Bermuda, to see my siblings again, but now I accepted there was little chance of that. So I began to dream of other lands, other adventures. Perhaps it was time for me to explore the world, if I could. Whenever I had the chance, I still chanted to myself those powerful words, "*Freedom!*" and "*Run!*"

That night, after returning home to the Darrell household, I plucked up the courage to ask the master, "I have heard news of a Mr John Wood soon to be travelling to Antigua. Might you let me travel under his service?"

I clenched my fists behind my back, hoping with all my heart that he would agree to my request.

Amazingly, he did agree! I couldn't believe my luck. I still, to this day, have no idea why he said yes. Whether he had been drinking, or simply was sick of the sight of me, I don't know – but God Himself was surely on my side that day.

So, Mr Wood bought me from Mr Darrell, whose wife had convinced him, telling him how hard-working and willing I was. Perhaps Master Darrell's years of ill treatment of me weighed on his conscience, because I heard that Master Darrell requested that I only be sold on to those who would 'not treat me ill'.

Since he himself treated me so badly over the years, I could only think that he had finally repented his behaviour, and for that I am thankful. I hoped that whoever worked for him in future would be treated more favourably than me, because I would not wish such cruelty on my worst enemy.

Mr and Mrs Wood lived in the town of St. John's, Antigua. Although they were not as physically cruel as Mr Darrell, occasionally beatings did occur. A little while after I arrived, I became sick and could barely walk. I worried that they might send me back to Mr Darrell, so I carried on with my chores as best I could, sitting down as I scrubbed and cleaned.

"The pain comes from years of standing in the salt ponds," I explained to the other slaves as I hobbled about. Some of them grumbled that I sat so often, but when I showed them my sores and scars, most of them felt sorry for me. But in truth, I was not much use as a worker for quite a while.

Mrs Greene lived in the next yard. She sent her own slave to help me, and for weeks she treated my wounds and aching limbs, rubbing them down with bark from a bush, which she'd boiled in hot water.

"This will help," she told me.

Gradually, over the years, the sores healed a little and walking was not as painful. Through all this suffering, I knew that God was by my side, guiding me through. I could still appreciate the beauty of His world; the sight of flowers blooming through the seasons, and the sweet sounds of birdsong or the murmuring wind.

One morning, I was called into the study by Mrs Wood.

"We are going away," she said. "I trust you to look after our home. Make sure that all is in order when we return."

I could barely contain my excitement! The other slaves had told me of how free and easy life was when they weren't being watched and scolded, and I could not wait to see this for myself.

I waved the Woods off. As soon as their horse and carriage disappeared from view, I ran through the house, singing, dancing and laughing in relief, knowing now that I had several weeks to myself.

That afternoon, I found a quiet room and dared to lie down on a soft bed, falling straight to sleep. When I woke, I had no idea what time it was, I only knew that I felt deeply, truly rested. My heart felt lighter and my mind clearer, and even my legs burned less. It was as if I were a young woman again!

"Good morning!" I greeted everyone as I strolled through the neighbourhood. "Please, I am available for extra work – if you need washing done, I will do it for a small sum."

As long as I looked after the Woods' household, I was allowed to take on small jobs to save money of my own. I knew it might take time, but eventually, I hoped, I would have enough money to buy my own freedom.

A few days later I was down at the seashore, laden with baskets of home-grown produce.

"Good morrow, captains!" I called gaily. "Would you care to buy yams or sweet potatoes? I have coffee too!"

The sailors, tired and hungry after their long journeys, were eager to buy my goods. In those hours, with my feet sinking into the sand and the sun at my back, I almost forgot I was a slave; I felt like a free woman. With the money I made, I bought hogs from a ship. Then I sold them for twice the price inland. Opportunities were plentiful when one was free!

Chapter 13

Antigua

1826–1828

Up to that time, I had not been much to church. I had been baptized years ago by an English reverend, but when I asked my master at the time to give me permission to attend Sunday school, he refused. I did not argue my case, for although I remembered a service or two from my days with Betsey, and carried the Lord in my heart, the way my life had revealed itself did not give me much cause for rejoicing.

But one Christmas, the Woods decided to take a trip to Date Hill, and I went along to look after the children. During our stay, I managed to find time to attend a Methodist church meeting on a nearby plantation called Winthorps.

I was greatly moved by all I saw and heard that evening. These were the first prayers I ever really listened to and understood.

Once we returned home, I decided to find a church I could join. I didn't tell a soul because I knew Mrs Wood would not allow me to attend. She cared only about working me so hard that I practically dropped dead each evening – she wouldn't be interested in my need to broaden my mind and unburden my soul. But from what I'd experienced at Date Hill, I knew the Lord had mighty power. The warmth and acceptance I'd felt at the Methodist meeting was balm for my wounded spirit. I was determined to find my way into the house of the Lord.

Soon, I got my chance. When I had walked the Wood children to school, I had noticed a church on the route.

"Now children," I said one morning when I was feeling brave. "Here is your lunch." I handed the children their pails. After I'd watched them enter the schoolyard, I ran to the nearby church.

I hovered by the open door. If the Woods found out, I would be flogged worse than ever before – not because they weren't churchgoing people, but because they did not permit us slaves to worship. They claimed that we could do that in our 'own time', but they knew well enough that we had no time of our own. Our every moment was taken up with their demands. But still, I needed to hear words more important and wiser than any I could say; I ached to be with people whose hope shone from them as if torches lit them from within.

"Welcome, dear," said a gentle voice. A woman smiled as I stood, twisting my hands hesitantly. "Come into the Lord's house."

Wooden benches lined the small hall, which was full of people. Many of them were now free – they were easy to recognize because they had fewer scars and injuries. Their faces were not as lined and pained. They carried themselves taller and their eyes were brighter. Looking at them gave me hope that one day I could call myself free too.

"I am Mrs Richter," the woman told me. "We are learning to read here, and all are welcome."

I soon discovered that I was a quick learner. I felt as if my mind had been a desert, waiting to be watered with knowledge. Seeing how seemingly random marks and shapes on a page translated to meaningful ideas made me glad to be alive each day. And as the weeks passed, I understood more and more.

One day as I sat reading a Bible passage, I heard a low, rich voice say, "Hello, miss."

I glanced up and saw a handsome face staring at me with the warmest, darkest eyes.

"I am Daniel," he said, smiling. I couldn't help noticing how smartly dressed he was!

"Hello, Daniel." I smiled shyly, my cheeks flushing. I looked down again at my books, but Daniel stood in the same spot, still looking at me.

"May I help you?" I asked, rather stiffly. His keen stare was making me uncomfortable. Even though we were in church, a holy place, I had seen many unholy things from the men and masters I had known. Although I had made some good male friends in my life, I wasn't used to being approached so directly, so I was rather guarded with him.

"You would help me very much if you would consider taking a walk with me. And I would like to ask your name, if I may."

"I am Mol…" I stopped. My name was not Molly. Molly was what my owners chose to call me. But here I was, talking with a handsome man who wanted to know my name. I drew myself up proudly and smiled as I said, "My name is Mary. Mary Prince."

I will always remember that first time I met Daniel. My heart beat faster, showing me how special this gentleman was. He was a *gentle man*.

"I would like very much to get to know you better, Mary Prince," said Daniel.

I blushed as I saw a tiny smile curling his top lip. I knew then that I had met my match, my love, and that looking into his eyes was like looking into a mirror.

Daniel James was a free Black man, a carpenter and cooper – making buckets and barrels to sell. He was honest, hardworking and a widower. He'd bought his freedom with money that he'd saved while he was a slave. He understood what being a slave was like. When I spoke of my scars and my shame, he held me tenderly while I cried.

It was nearly Christmas, and I was out walking with Daniel when he stopped and turned to me, his face questioning.

"Will you be my wife?" he asked me.

It was as if a bird inside my breast surged up and flew through my entire body. I gave him my best smile. "I might."

"On what does your decision depend?" He took hold of my hand, kissing the palm.

I whipped my hand away and laughed. "You should come to church with me."

"You forget, that's where I met you."

"You only came to learn reading," I said.

He took me into his arms. "And I ended up learning the language of love."

Daniel had certainly taught me how to feel love.

When we were out walking together, in those precious, snatched moments, I had glimpses of another, better life. A life where I could be free. Where I could think and do and say what I wanted, where I didn't have to live in fear of the next beating or unkind word.

Daniel and I were married by the Reverend Mr Olufsen in the Moravian Chapel at Spring Gardens. Free men were not allowed to marry enslaved women, so we couldn't marry in the English church. Although I knew my marriage was forbidden, my heart overruled my head. Even though my masters would be terribly displeased, it was wonderful to choose my own path for the first time ever.

Of course, word of my marriage quickly spread. That evening when I returned to the Woods' residence, both Mr and Mrs Wood shouted and screamed at me. They sent for Daniel, and my heart broke to hear how Mr Wood hollered at him.

"Who gave you the right to marry one of my slaves?" Mr Wood roared, his face turning purple.

"Sir, I am a free man. I thought I had a right to choose a wife. If I had known Mary wasn't allowed to have a husband, I would not have asked her to marry me, but I fell in love and my heart won out, sir."

Daniel kept his dignity and his temper. Hearing my

husband – a free man – defend his love for me and not cower at the hands of the white man was a wonderful thing to witness. He was so reasonable and respectful that Mr Wood had nothing much more to say about the matter. But Mrs Wood was still so angry that she practically frothed at the mouth. She begged Mr Wood to flog me, which of course he did. He always ended up doing what she wanted.

Mrs Wood wouldn't let up about Daniel. She declared that he wouldn't be allowed anywhere near the yard and he wasn't to ask me to wash his clothes. There were to be no signs of his existence in her household. She screamed at me that my time was her time, and I was not to spend one second of it doing anything for my husband.

I wanted to tell her that she'd had enough of my time, that she'd claimed half my life, but instead I broke down.

"Why don't you just sell me?" I wept. But she only set her lips in a tight grim line and shook her head.

"You'd like that, wouldn't you? To go somewhere else? Well, I am your mistress, and I will never let you go!"

I could not understand Mrs Wood. She only ever had unkind things to say about me and my work. She was happy to sell other slaves – so why not me?

One day, sitting in the shade of a calabash tree, Daniel and I spoke about our future and what we could do.

"My rheumatism is hurting me so," I said. The aches and pains in my joints made it painful to move them. Daniel bowed his head and knelt at my feet. He rubbed my legs and sighed.

"My house is comfortable, and I wish you could come and live with me in it."

I wished for that too. And even though I was not one for crying about things that can't be changed, I couldn't help shedding tears as my husband whispered sweetly to me, his soft hands rubbing my painful legs.

"I have heard rumours that the Woods are soon travelling to England," said Daniel.

I had heard about London, and how different life was there. The British parliament had made it against the law to buy or sell people into slavery by the 1807 Slave Trade Act, and many people there were arguing that slavery should be abolished completely.

My heart leapt at this news. With the Woods away, I might be able to spend more time with Daniel. But before I voiced these thoughts, he added, "I will miss you when you go, but perhaps the weather might help your rheumatism. And who knows? Perhaps Mr Wood will finally agree to sell you back your freedom if you can earn enough. You might return home a free woman!"

A free woman? The word *free* swam in my head so fast that it seemed to become a living, breathing thing. Me? A free woman? What would that mean? Here I was, forty years old, and all I had ever known was being in service to others. But now, as I looked into the eyes of the man I loved, to imagine returning home to him ... free? Well, that was the sweetest idea I could ever imagine.

Daniel smiled. I don't know exactly what that smile held – hope, I think. And love – I felt Daniel's love for me deep in my bones. I wanted so much to be able to walk and talk and laugh with him. But what I wanted more than anything else in the whole world was freedom. To be free is very sweet.

Chapter 14

London, England

Summer 1828

Although I was brought to London to look after the Woods' children, I spent most of my first few months washing clothes. After the Caribbean, England seemed a dreary and grey place. Even the birds that perched on the windowsills were grey. Huge, grey, stone buildings loomed over the pavements and the streets thundered with horses and carriages clattering by. I missed the vivid pink and purple flowers of Bermuda, the trees, the warm breeze, the air itself.

In London, the sun was not as warm as it was back home. And constantly having to dip my hands in hot then cold water did my rheumatism no good at all. Instead of feeling better, as Daniel had hoped, I felt myself become stiffer, achier and more unwell.

Mrs Wood had brought such heavy clothes too! Every

couple of months, when it was time for the great wash, she dumped heaps of mattress sacks and coverlets into my arms.

"Here, take these!"

I could barely move under the weight.

"Mistress," I began, hesitantly. I had worked for her for over thirteen years now, but I wanted to say my piece. "I am too sick to wash so many items. Please, can we think about a way that I might—"

She whirled round, quivering with rage.

"I suppose because we are in England now, you think yourself free, do you?" she said, her voice low and cruel. "Just because your kind are rebelling in Barbados and Demerara – and although we are not allowed buy new slaves, that law will not help you! You are still my property."

As she spoke, spittle flew from her lips and landed on my cheek. I wiped it away with my hand.

"You are not a free woman!" she yelled. "You are not free and never forget that!"

She marched up to me and shoved the bundles of washing out of my hands. We both gazed at the pile on the floor.

"If you do not pick up that washing and go and do it directly, then I shall have no choice but to turn you out into the street," she hissed.

She left the room and I stood there, staring at the laundry

at my feet. What should I do? They kept threatening to throw me out. I wanted so much to leave, but I didn't know these streets well enough yet, or have knowledge of the chances open to me. So I stayed. I had no choice.

As the days passed, I comforted myself as I worked by singing hymns that I remembered from church. I recited the thoughtful words that Daniel had said to me. How I longed to see his lovely face and be in his arms once again!

The other washerwomen I met were usually pleasant, and sometimes they even did my tasks for me when I struggled. As we worked, the women would discuss the new laws about slavery that had been passed in the British parliament. At home, I nervously enquired about my freedom. Impatiently, Mr Woods dashed his newspaper to one side.

"If you don't do the washing as you're told, I will send you to the brig in the river or back to Antigua! Or perhaps you'd like to be out on the streets, eh? Let's see how you get on then!"

Mr Wood fetched the horsewhip, meaning to use it on me.

I flung myself to my knees. "I would willingly go back – if only you grant me my freedom!" I pleaded.

The mention of freedom made him even angrier. "Stop asking for your freedom!" he roared, striking the horsewhip against the back of the chair. Hearing the *thwack!* I cowered, fearing I would be next.

Mr Wood marched up and down, kicking the furniture and cursing to himself, taking the Lord's name in vain. I told him that I had heard slavery was not allowed now in England, but he just laughed bitterly.

"And how do you think you'd survive? You're getting old – you're practically lame! What work will you find? You have no references, no one will hire you. You will die of cold! How ungrateful you are! Here you have food and a place to sleep, but still you do nothing but wail and moan!"

He stormed out, and I sat on the floor and wept. His words were like poison arrows that pierced my heart. I needed to think. I was in London, and here I *could* be free! I should be brave and bold and stop thinking that I could never be free. But where could I go? How might I earn my living?

Life became even harder for me after the cook and other staff left the Woods' employ. When I slept, I would often have nightmares about wandering the dark London streets, alone and injured. One night, I dreamed of my own death. As I lay on a cobbled street, gasping my final breaths, I had a vision of my dear mother. Her voice was soothing, and her breath warmed my frozen cheeks.

"Do not wait for freedom to come in death, Mary Prince," she said. "Take your chance now, while your heart still beats in your brave, bold, broken body."

I woke in a cold sweat, tears on my face. But I felt a peace settle over me. The Lord protected and watched over me; He always had and always would.

After a lifetime of hopelessness, it was sometimes difficult to keep hope alive in my heart. But I was starting to believe that things could change. Sunshine and blue sky, rustling leaves, chirping birds and children's laughter – all this reminded me of the goodness in life. The Lord's way was not a life of humiliation and hurt.

I decided there and then that I would no longer be imprisoned; it was time to trust in the Lord and His will.

Chapter 15

London, England

Autumn 1828

We had been living in London for about three months and the Woods had threatened to turn me out on the streets four times. I had worked out that this new threat was just another way to torment me; they knew how much the idea of being alone on unfamiliar streets frightened me.

Over the years, the Woods had continually beaten and yelled at me. They had made me feel worthless and useless in so many different ways. And now that my life of hard work had left me sick and in pain, they no longer thought I was useful to them. But I still had life in me – lots of it! I felt as strong as ever in my mind and I wanted so much to return to my beloved Daniel. I would stand this treatment no longer! Slavery was not law here – finally, things were changing for the better and ordinary people were realizing that slavery was evil. I made a decision.

At the Woods', I was packing my things, my heart feeling lighter than it had in years, when Mrs Pell, a friend of the Woods, came to visit. Mrs Wood had asked her to speak to me.

"Are you really going to leave?"

I nodded, afraid to speak in case my voice cracked; I didn't want to show how nervous I was. I wouldn't go back on my decision; I wouldn't let doubts creep into my mind.

"Don't leave. How about coming out to the country with me? The fresh air will do you the world of good!"

I knew that my master and mistress had asked her to persuade me to stay. They wanted her to weaken my determination to be a free woman.

For a moment, the idea of country air and rolling green hills appealed to me, but I understood how Mrs Wood's mind worked. She thought a break in the country would get me back under her control. But the idea that I could walk the streets a free woman had given me a glimpse into what my world could look like. Now that I had imagined that possibility, no one was going to snatch it away from me.

"I can no longer stand to be so used," I told Mrs Pell.

As I continued to gather my things, I could hear Mrs Wood loudly telling everyone about all the terrible things that would happen to me if I left. She didn't dare to say these things to my face, but she wanted me to hear them. She was trying to frighten me.

But it was Mrs Wood who was frightened, not me. She did not care about me; she was a selfish, bossy woman who was only concerned with having a slave as reliable and dedicated as I had been all these years.

Mr Wood wanted to make it as hard as possible for me to find a new job. He gave me papers that stated I had come to London of my own free will and that I was leaving by my own free will – and also that I was bone idle and refused to work.

The nurse and servant girls watched, wide-eyed, as I dragged my trunk through the kitchen. I wanted to make it clear that I was choosing to go – I was not being dismissed. I knew the wicked lies Mrs Wood would tell once I left.

With my head held high, even though my voice wobbled, I said to them all, "I have always worked my hardest to please my owners, but you must understand – there is no pleasing some people. They will work you until you bleed and then bleed you more. I told them I was sick. I begged for mercy and was given none. And so, now I am leaving, and I want it to be known that I have done no wrong."

When I opened the heavy door, I trembled at what I was

about to do. This morning, I was going to walk through London as a free woman! I practically flew down the street. I was relieved and glad of my decision. Decent and caring people did exist, I just had to trust that I would find them!

I took myself to where a man called Mash lived. Mash used to shine the family's shoes. We had often chatted together, and he had always been full of good humour.

"Mary!" He smiled when he opened the door. "To what do I owe this pleasure?"

"Might I ask if your wife knows of anyone who could take me to Hatton Garden?"

"What's your business there?" he asked, curious.

"I want to visit the missionaries," I replied. The washerwomen had told me about the Moravian Mission House in Hatton Garden and my plan was to go there and ask them to help me. Mash's wife sent a young girl to take me to the mission house. Once there, I spoke to a gentleman called Mr Moore. As I told him the sorry tale of my life with the Woods, Mr Moore listened sympathetically.

"Can you help me, sir?" I asked. I was frightened and desperate. I knew that if I had to go back to the Woods, I'd be beaten badly and made to regret my bid for freedom.

I needn't have worried. He welcomed me warmly.

"I am so sorry to hear of your situation," he said, kindly.

"Perhaps between us we can think of a way out. Meanwhile, you may bring your trunk here and leave it with us under our care, if you wish."

I begged Mash and his wife to take me in. They did, generously. I had a little Caribbean money that I'd brought with me, and they helped me to change it into British pounds. This would keep me going for a little while, at least.

I rested at Mash's house for a few months. They found me a doctor who gave me medicine that helped ease the pain from my rheumatism. I slept so much that sometimes Mrs Mash wondered if I would ever wake up; I was making up for all the years that I had been unable to rest properly. My strength began to return and, feeling better, I asked Mash's wife if I could help her around the house.

The Lord bestowed His grace on me, and instead of nightmares of dying and suffering, my dreams instead were of soaring blissfully over turquoise seas. Daniel's face often appeared in these dreams. I sometimes woke with my arms squeezing a cushion! *Oh Daniel, to be free is so sweet,* I whispered to myself over and over. And it was.

But I needed to think about my future: I had no permanent roof over my head, I could scarcely read and write, and my pain meant I was not as quick and nimble as I had once been. What was to be next for me?

Chapter 16

London, England

June 1829

In spite of all the uncertainty, these were happy days for me!

At last, there was light and possibility in my life. I had a place of refuge – a place where decent men and women lived by their honourable beliefs. A lady from the church called Mrs Hill told me about the Anti-Slavery Society and said we should go and see them.

At their offices, as I sat and drank sweet tea, Mrs Hill explained, "I don't know how much you know, dear, but even though the Abolition Act was passed, and the law doesn't recognize slavery in Britain, *nothing* has been done about those poor enslaved people who are still working in the colonies of our empire! No one has freed them."

"Why not?" I asked. "If the law was passed in 1807, why is it taking so long?"

"It is not so simple. Plantation owners, powerful men, have written pamphlets to persuade people that the slave trade is still needed. They say that our country's prosperity relies on slavery – and they try to scare people by claiming that Britain would collapse without it. They use their power to put pressure on the government. But, freeing all slaves everywhere – that's what we're working towards now."

"Working towards?" I asked.

"Yes, there are huge numbers of us abolitionists, campaigning and writing to parliament."

"When will the slaves be freed?" I asked, my voice hopeful, images of my sisters and brothers flooding my mind.

She shook her head, frowning. "The society has been campaigning for five years now. Progress is slower than we'd wish, but we're growing in numbers. It's not only the church that's behind this movement, but important politicians and powerful men too."

Now I understood. The law said that I was free in Britain, but if I went back to Antigua, I'd still be a slave.

"Do you know someone who could help me?" I asked. Perhaps they might have the funds to send me back. Even if I were still a slave there, at least I would be with my sweet Daniel again!

"We will go to Thomas Pringle," she said, smiling. "He is the secretary of the Anti-Slavery Society and knows a great many things on this matter. I do not think your troubles are over yet, Mary dear. Let us go and see Thomas and see what he says."

As we set off, she told me about two famous ex-slaves who had spoken out about their experiences, Ottobah Cugoano and Olaudah Equiano. She told me that Olaudah toured around England, Ireland and Scotland, sharing his story. Ottobah had published an essay called *Thoughts and Sentiments on the Evil of Slavery* in 1787. I was amazed. To think that he was speaking of these things a full year before I was even born! I had never heard of either of these men, yet they had been fighting the good fight for more than forty years, telling ordinary people about the reality of being a slave. No longer could anyone pretend that there was anything good about slavery.

My heart stung when I thought of all the people I had left behind, still toiling at their tasks, picking cotton or tobacco, or labouring in those horrible salt ponds – injured, separated from their loved ones, dying. I was glad that these men were telling British people of the horrors that were being done in their name, in their colonies across the seas. What brutal lives those of us with darker skin were being forced to lead!

We made our way to Mr Pringle's office in Aldermanbury, East London. It was November now and I had never felt anything as bitterly cold as an English winter. The icy wind sliced through my thin clothing – I felt as if I would never be warm again.

The office was in an imposing, impressive granite building that had stood for many years. I listened while Mrs Hill spoke to Thomas Pringle and other men about what could be done for me. Suggestions and ideas danced around the room like butterflies: was it possible to send me back to the Caribbean as a free woman?

We spent days going back and forth to the office; it made my head spin to try and understand the language these men were using. It seemed no one could agree on the best thing to do; I was free according to the laws in England but if I went back to Antigua, I would still be the Woods' property.

Now that I no longer needed to toil for Mr and Mrs Wood, I felt a sense of freedom, but I still wasn't fully free. I was far from my beautiful home country, with its palm trees and bluebirds. I was far from seeing myself on those sunny streets. I couldn't be in Daniel's arms; I couldn't lift my voice to the Lord at my church. I hadn't had any children of my own – my masters had ensured that would never be a prospect. My body was broken by unending work. These men, these laws, had taken more than just my freedom!

Mr Pringle took me to see Mr George Stephen, who he said was an expert on the laws of property and slavery.

"I am a solicitor," Mr Stephen told me. "I will examine your case to discover whether or not we can legally obtain your freedom for you to return to Antigua."

"Oh, sir!" I cried excitedly. "If I could return home as a free woman – all my suffering will fade from my mind, even though scars may remain on my body! But, to go home and be considered a slave still? No, I would rather go to my grave!"

Back at Mash's house, I paced the floor, fretting about how long it might take for my freedom to be granted. I was worried about running out of money, but the church and the Anti-Slavery Society gave me a little to tide me over.

"We visited Mr Wood," one of the anti-slavery men told me. "We asked him if he would allow you to return to your husband as a free woman, but he refused."

"That doesn't surprise me," I replied, remembering Mr Wood's stubborn temper and foolish pride. He did not want me to be free, and more than that, he didn't want me to be happy. I will never understand where this callousness came from; he saw slaves not as people but only as possessions.

"We were surprised at his refusal," the man added. "We offered him a reasonably large sum of money and assumed that…" He looked down without finishing.

I didn't reply but could have told him that Mr Wood's unholy ideas could never be changed by money. There was no way, if Mr Wood could help it, that I would ever be free.

Soon after this, Mash entered the kitchen where I was cooking and told me that a woman was at the door, asking for me. I did not know many people and wondered who it might be.

A small woman with a large bag in her arms smiled at me. "I am from the Quakers," she said.

I knew that the Quakers, like the Moravians, were against slavery.

"We know that you are not used to this climate," she said. "It gets so cold here in the winter – you might even get to see snow! We have collected some clothes which will help to keep you warm."

She laid the bag at my feet, and I dropped to my knees and raked through the items. Tears of gratitude came to my eyes as I felt the thickness and warmth of the skirts and dresses.

"Thank you for your kindness," I said as I wiped away

my tears. "I am most grateful. But I do not wish to be idle. If you or your friends know of work that needs doing, please tell me so that I can earn a living and be of use in society. I do not wish to eat the bread of idleness."

She left, promising that if she heard of anything suitable, she would let me know.

Chapter 17

London, England

1830

A little while later, Mrs Mash found me work as a cleaner for a very respectable lady, who paid me quite well. I gave some of my wages to Mr and Mrs Mash for my rent and upkeep. Even though they did not have much money themselves, they had never allowed me to go hungry or asked me to leave when I was ill.

Christmas came and went. My bones gradually became more used to the cold. Through the early months of the following year, I even came to enjoy the crispness of the air, that fresh bite that awoke you instantly. I carried on working, but I heard no more news about my freedom.

As the spring flowers bloomed in London's parks and gardens, I was lucky enough to be offered work by a woman called Mrs Forsyth. She asked if I would like to go with her to clean, wash and do general chores.

Mr Mash reminded me how useful it would be for my cause if I had good references from other employers, seeing as Mr Wood had provided me with nothing helpful.

"I live near the sea," Mrs Forsyth said. "I used to live in the Caribbean, so I know how well you people can work."

Thinking of the lapping waves and vastness of the ocean back home, I agreed in a heartbeat. I wondered what the ocean here looked like. Would it be the same?

The town Mrs Forsyth lived in was called Margate. I spent a happy six months there and it almost makes me weep to think of how good it felt to be treated fairly and reasonably. Yes, I worked long hours, but I was never struck, or spoken to unkindly. I felt I was a valued member of Mrs Forsyth's household. All those years I wasted, giving my unforgiving masters the best of me when they offered nothing of the kind in return. I wish that I had worked a fraction as hard for them; they would never have known!

When Mrs Forsyth had to go travelling on business, my employment with her came to an end.

I found myself lodgings for two shillings a week and managed to afford candles and coal, but after a few weeks, my money ran out. I returned to the Anti-Slavery office.

"I need to work," I explained to Mr Pringle. "Work is all I know. I wish to contribute, to be useful."

Working keeps the hands busy, the mind from wandering and the heart from longing. Whenever I had time to myself, sadness overwhelmed me. I missed Daniel. I wondered if my siblings were alive. I didn't wish to dwell on such unhappy things.

"Would you consider becoming part of our household?" Mr Pringle asked me. The smile on my face gave him his answer!

It turned out to be the best position I could have hoped for, in this country far away from those I loved.

"Come, Mary," Mrs Pringle said one summer day. "Put down your scrubbing brush. It's time for your Bible lessons."

We sat next to one another at the table, a Bible open in front of us. The warm sunshine shone on my face as Mrs Pringle explained the Lord's prayers. I repeated them back to her, warmth and restoration spreading through my ageing bones.

The Reverend Young lived next door to the Pringles and he was a very thoughtful man. I attended church three times every Sunday, and the comfort I received there kept my spirits up.

Between the Reverend Young and the Reverend

Mortimer, whose ministry I belonged to, I was now familiar with the Bible. I listened to their sermons, and although I appreciated the message, I found it hard to forgive. They told me that I must learn forgiveness, that I should keep my heart open, but they were not the ones with scars covering every inch of their body, with limbs that ached constantly.

If I could have simply forgotten the hardships I had suffered, then of course I would have – but things were not as simple as these white folk believed. I understood that they did not wish to linger on the mistakes and wrongdoing of their fellow men, but if we are to learn, we must face up to what has gone on before, and examine why these things happened. If a child doesn't learn that fire is hot, then they are destined to burn themselves over and over again.

I had been a slave my entire life. For over thirty of those years, I endured misery that most people would not wish on their worst enemies! And yet, I was still expected to be gentle and humble. I did not feel humble! I did not feel quiet. Part of me wished to rage, rage, rage against the world's injustices. People speak of progress and industry, but how can there be true progress when one man still has power over another, just because of the colour of their skin?

I knew that I must leave the question of my freedom to others to decide, but I longed to be free, and I knew it was my right. I trusted the good Lord to find a way to give me my liberty and guide me back to Daniel's loving arms, where I belonged.

After many long discussions, Mr Pringle suggested that if more ordinary folk were to be made aware of the realities of slave life, then it might help the anti-slavery cause. He said that if I told the full, detailed story of my life, no matter how horrible, it might open people's eyes to the truth of what was still happening around the world.

At first, I was against his plan. I preferred to keep silent about my own struggles – partly because I thought it would be better to try to forget them, and partly because I hated the idea of drawing attention to myself.

But Mr Pringle reminded me of all the good men and women of England who were taking up the cause of abolition, including the new prime minister, Lord Grenville, who believed in the cause and promoted abolitionists in parliament. Mr Pringle also told me about the case of Jonathan Strong, a slave who had been freed by the English courts with the help of an Englishman called Granville Sharp. And finally, he convinced me when he told me of the tragedy of the *Zong*. And what a tragedy it was!

The *Zong* was a ship that carried African slaves to the Americas. In 1781, the ship ran into bad weather and had to spend three extra days at sea. The supplies ran out – so the crew threw 131 slaves overboard. They murdered them. Mr Pringle explained the horrific truth. The slaves were considered by the law as goods, not people. If they had died on the ship, the ship owners would not have received any money. But by throwing the slaves off the ship, the owners could claim compensation from their insurers for goods lost at sea.

Chapter 18

London, England –
Mr Pringle's Household

1830

So, here I am. I have decided that I will help Mr Pringle show the world why slavery is the worst of evils. Who better, he says, to tell the story than a woman who has experienced so many atrocities first-hand? Mr Pringle says British people are hungry to hear the voices of enslaved Africans and those whose ancestors came from Africa, and that I will be the first woman to tell her story.

"You are unique!" he tells me, smiling.

I know.

Today, over two hundred branches of the Anti-Slavery Society exist in England. Mr Pringle says that William Wilberforce and Lord Brougham, important men with high-powered jobs in government, are talking about us in parliament. Protests are growing. A few years ago, the Demerara rebellion broke out. Slave masters had been told by the British government to free their slaves, and when they did not, over twelve thousand slaves protested.

Those who wish to end slavery are called abolitionists, and the cause has a growing number of members. When Mr Pringle named them all it made me feel quite giddy! As well as the Anti-Slavery Society, there is the Methodist Society, the British and Foreign Bible Society, the Baptist Missionary Society, the London Missionary Society and the Church Missionary Society.

Mr Pringle says that most ordinary folk have no idea about the reality of slavery. They have been fed lies that we are all treated well and are happy and grateful. Some people believe that many of us do not even have our own minds! He says that many people will change their minds when they read my story.

It *is* up to slaves like me to explain and educate people. I have heard people say that slaves do not want to be free. It's easy to believe what we are told by those in power, or those who we think have more knowledge or influence than us. But I would ask every ordinary man and woman to challenge their own thinking. How can a slave be happy with a whip on their back? Separated from their families and bought and sold and like cattle?

The British like to think of themselves as civilized, well-mannered and polite – but their behaviour thousands of miles from home shows this is not true. All their decency disappears when there is a profit to be made by using us to do their backbreaking tasks.

And so, I will tell my story. I am about to sit down now, and Mrs Strickland, who is a writer herself, has agreed to write down what I say, with Mr Pringle's help. Then they will read it back to me and we will decide on which words to keep in and which to take out.

"Mary, come," says Mr Pringle. "Make yourself comfortable. We are ready for you to begin. Tell us your story."

THE END

But what happened after
Mary wrote her book?

Mary's book, *The History of Mary Prince, A West Indian Slave, Related by Herself*, was published in February 1831. Mary was forty-three years old. This time in British history was known as the Georgian period, after kings George I, II, III and IV, who ruled from 1714–1830. By writing her book, Mary helped the abolitionist cause. When the British public heard the stories of real enslaved people, they realized just how inhumane slavery really was. Ordinary people hadn't understood what was going on. And those who did understand were getting so rich from the profits of slavery that they didn't want it to end.

Enslaved men had told their stories before, but Mary is so important to our history because she was the first Black woman to give an account of her experiences. As with anyone sharing their story, we need to appreciate that Mary verbally told her life story to another woman who wrote it down. Then the story was edited by Thomas Pringle.

It's a little like when you tell someone about something that happened to you and then they tell someone else; each time the story is told, some details might be left out or changed.

Mary's book had a huge effect. In 1831 it sold out and a further two editions were printed, which shows how popular it was. Readers were interested in hearing direct accounts from slaves who were dispelling the myths around slavery. The tide was turning!

Thomas Pringle quoted Mary's book in parliament to gain support and put pressure on MPs to change the laws. Her autobiography especially struck a chord with female anti-slavery campaigners. Mary's account emphasized how slavery ruined people's lives – in particular, how it broke up families.

Mary's book caused a fuss, and soon after it came out there were a series of civil lawsuits: in *Blackwood's Magazine*, a man called Thomas Cadell published pro-slavery attacks on Mary and Thomas Pringle. This led to Pringle suing Cadell in 1833. Mary briefly took the stand as a witness in the court case – this is the only known record of her words, apart from in her autobiography.

Mr Wood also sued Pringle for libel (writing untrue accusations). Pringle couldn't provide any real-life witnesses from the Caribbean to confirm the terrible things that

Mary Prince had said that Mr Wood had done, so Wood won his case. That court case is the last time that there is any public record of Mary. After 1833, we lose track of her.

In August 1833, a law called the Slavery Abolition Act was passed. This meant that all slaves in the Caribbean were free – although slaves working in some other British colonies around the world still were not.

Acts of parliament can be very complicated, and this one was especially complex. One section said that ex-slaves still had to work for their masters. So even though slaves were now technically free, this meant that they still had to work for their masters, and that now they would be called 'apprentices' and paid a small amount of money. Obviously, the Act didn't mean that the masters suddenly become kind employers! Ill treatment still happened. People were against this apprenticeship scheme and there were many protests. Queen Victoria came to the British throne in 1837. By then, views on slavery had changed.

Thankfully, in 1838, more than 750,000 British slaves were freed. This time, slavery really was abolished. This Act meant that Mary would have been able to return to Antigua as a free woman! Of course, the slave owners weren't happy about losing their workers – and their profits. So Britain paid them £20 million in compensation – in today's money, the sum would be £25.3 billion, and tax payers only stopped paying for this 'compensation' in 2015. Instead of compensating the people who had been enslaved and treated so brutally for years, the government instead rewarded the plantation owners who'd owned the slaves. In the National Archives there are records and files. They tell you all about the slave owners – as well as other information, such as how many slaves they owned and where they lived.

Across the Atlantic Ocean in America, slavery only came to an end much later – in 1865.

Author's Note

I'm forty-six years old and was born in Cardiff, Wales. I moved around a lot when I was younger because I was brought up in children's homes and foster homes. Because I didn't have any choice over who I lived with or where I went, ideas around freedom have always been very important to me.

When we learn about terrible events that have happened throughout history, and even in the world today – at the time of writing this, there is a war in Ukraine – I believe that we can better understand the world, and more importantly each other, if we think about those issues that may make us feel a little uncomfortable or sad. If we want to change things, then we need to talk about those issues – they're important. If we don't say how we feel, or ask questions, then how will anyone know things need to change?

We need to walk our streets and look at our land with fresh eyes. If you come from Liverpool or Lancashire and learn about the role the docks played in the transatlantic slave trade or learn how local communities were impacted by the cotton famine, it can make you feel more connected to where you and your family have come from. The more we understand about how and why we got somewhere, the better our chances are of not repeating the same mistakes in the future.

Back to Mary Prince – the sad truth is that we have no idea what happened to her after about 1833. We don't even know what she looked like because no pictures or photographs of her exist. If you search her name online, images do come up, but these are images of other Black women at the time; they are not Mary.

The optimistic side of me hopes that Mary had a much happier end to her life. I love to imagine her on a ship back to Antigua where, at the shore, she runs into Daniel's arms and spends the remaining years of her life enjoying her country as a free woman. But the reality is that we don't know. And, even when slavery had 'officially' ended, it was a long time before life became fair for many previously enslaved Black people.

Unfortunately, we all know that racism and prejudice still exist today.

Gaining knowledge is necessary for change. If you don't know something, then you could ask your parents or whoever looks after you. If they don't know, perhaps you could make it a mission to discover the answer together! There are also teachers or librarians. They will be able to guide you to the right places to do some research. The 'Further Reading' section of this book would make a great start.

In some ways, I wish I were back at school. I loved history, but all I remember learning about was Henry VIII and his wives, and the Holocaust in the Second World War. I enjoyed dressing up as an Egyptian and a Roman. But I never saw any pictures or heard about any Black or Brown people in the history I was taught or in the stories I read. I didn't live with anyone who knew about these things either because I was always fostered in white households. Any time I expressed an interest in finding out anything different, I wasn't encouraged.

I had never heard of the race riots in 1919, or the Windrush generation's arrival in 1948, or the Notting Hill riots in the 1980s. Not knowing people like me existed made me feel invisible; if you feel invisible, you can start to feel that you don't matter. But we all matter.

Nowadays, schools are different, and thankfully, you'll know about many wonderful Black and Brown people who've influenced and contributed to our British history – people like Ignatius Sancho, Olaudah Equiano and Sarah Forbes Bonetta – and that's fantastic! But we can't ignore the past or pretend certain things didn't happen. It's a little bit like if you break something – even if it was an accident, the right thing to do is to own up, isn't it? You always feel better once you've apologized. It's the same for our country. We need to hold up our hands and say, "Sorry we made these mistakes, but we will learn for next time," because that is how things change.

It's amazing to believe how different life is for us now, how much has changed over the past few hundred years: LGBTQ+ people used to be imprisoned, women couldn't vote, and Black people were thought of as property and even paraded in "zoos" for entertainment. It's a very good thing that life isn't like that any more, but terrible things still happen all across the globe, and slavery still exists.

It's worth finding out how *you* can change things and become aware of what is going on in your world. You can join organizations to help save the planet, ensure fair conditions for workers, stop cruelty to animals and end racism. You (and your family and friends) can sign petitions, write to MPs and go on marches – none of these things cost money, they just take a little time. We've seen what Greta Thunberg has achieved by standing up for what she believes in. Well, it's never too early to think about what *you* believe in.

Even if history changes, people's hopes and wishes don't. Although two hundred years separate Mary and me, we both believe in the same things: equality for all and the right of every person to be free.

I'm privileged to have read her story and I am glad to have this chance to bring her life to you. She, as well as hundreds of thousands of others, deserves to be remembered.

E.L. Norry, April 2022

Granville Sharp and Jonathan Strong

In 1765, Jonathan Strong, an enslaved Black man, was beaten by his master, David Lisle, and left in the streets. Jonathan was nearly dead but managed to make his way to the house of William Sharp, a doctor, who gave free medical help to the poor people in London. Granville Sharp lived with his brother, and together the brothers helped Strong with food and money and took him to hospital. It took more than four months for Jonathan to recover from his injuries. After his recovery, his master tried to recapture him, but Granville took Lisle to court. Granville argued that because Jonathan was now in England, he wasn't a slave any more. But it wasn't until 1768 that the courts agreed with Granville and Jonathan was freed. The case became very famous, and Granville used this in his campaigning work to end slavery.

Ottobah Cugoano

Ottobah Cugoano was born around 1757 in Africa. He was kidnapped by slave traders as a young boy. In 1786, he contacted Granville Sharp about helping a Black man, Henry Demane, who'd been kidnapped and was about to be shipped to the Caribbean. Granville managed to rescue Henry before the ship left. In 1787, with the help of Olaudah Equiano, Ottobah published a book about his own experiences in *Thoughts and Sentiments on the Evil and Wicked Traffic of the Slavery and Commerce of the Human Species*. He called for an end to the slave trade and freedom for all slaves.

Olaudah Equiano

Olaudah Equiano was born in 1745 in Nigeria. Aged eleven, he was kidnapped along with his sister and sold into slavery. He was sold many times, eventually being taken to the Caribbean, where he bought his own freedom. In 1782 he brought the *Zong* massacre to Granville Sharp's attention. He wrote his autobiography, *The Interesting Narrative of the Life of Olaudah Equiano, Or Gustavus Vassa, The African,* in 1789. It was one of the earliest first-hand accounts of what it was actually like being enslaved.

Glossary

Osnaburg – a cheap, coarse, woven fabric most commonly used in making clothes for slaves

Abolition Act of 1807 – the act which ended the buying and selling of slaves within the British Empire, however it did not stop slave owners from being able to keep their existing enslaved people

Abolition Act of 1833 – the act which abolished slavery in most British colonies including the Caribbean

Abolitionists – people who wanted to abolish, or end, slavery

Anti-Slavery Society – a group committed to ending slavery, formed in 1823

Civil lawsuit – when two people or organizations ask a court or judge to solve a disagreement between them

Colony – a country or geographical area which is ruled by another person, country or government. *See* Empire.

Cotton famine – a significant era of poverty and unemployment in the textile communities of Lancashire from 1861–65 caused by a blockade on raw cotton from America

Empire – a group of lands or colonies under the control of a powerful person, country or government who conquered them. *See* Colony.

Methodism – a branch of Protestant Christianity that believes that people should have a personal relationship with God. *See* Protestant.

Moravians – a branch of Protestant Christianity that stresses the importance of community. *See* Protestant.

MP or Member of Parliament – the person who has been elected to represent the people who live in a particular area

Overseer – a person who supervised slaves

Privateersman – an officer or commander of a privateer, an armed ship

Protestant – a Christian who belongs to a church other than the Catholic Church or an Eastern Orthodox church

Provision ground – land set aside for slaves to grow their own food

Quakers – members of the Christian group known as the Society of Friends who believe in peace and oppose slavery

Royal Navy – the United Kingdom's military ship organization

Slave – a person who is owned by another and is forced to follow orders and work for them without being paid

Slave owner – a person who owns one or more slaves and forces them to work. *See* Slave.

Slave trade – the capturing, selling and buying of people

Sloop – a type of sailing boat

Solicitor – a type of British lawyer

Sugar plantation – a large area of land where sugar is grown and harvested

Switch – a long, thin branch from a tree used to hit people

Trading ship – a large boat used to carry items for sale

Yellow-wood – a type of tree

Further Reading

Books

books marked with an asterisk (*) are suitable for
younger readers

Boakye, Jeffrey, *Black, Listed: Black British Culture Explored*
ISBN 9780349700564

Gerzina, Gretchen, *Black Victorians/Black Victoriana*
ISBN 9780813532158

*Hammond, Alison, and Norry, E.L., *Black in Time:
The Most Awesome Black Britons from Yesterday to Today*
ISBN 9780241532317

*Hepburn, Judy, *My Story: Ignatius Sancho*
ISBN 9781407199573

*McKissack, Patricia C., *My Story: A Picture of Freedom*
ISBN 9780702303814

Olusoga, David, *Black and British: A Forgotten History*
ISBN 9781447299769

Prince, Mary, *The History of Mary Prince, A West
Indian Slave* ISBN 9798526589062

Saini, Angela, *Superior: The Return of Race Science* ISBN 9780008293864

Vernon, Patrick, and Osborne, Angelina, *100 Great Black Britons* ISBN 9781472144300

Walker, Robin, *Black History Matters* ISBN 9781445166896

Website

www.maryprince.org

Experience history first-hand with My Story – a series of vividly imagined accounts of life in the past.

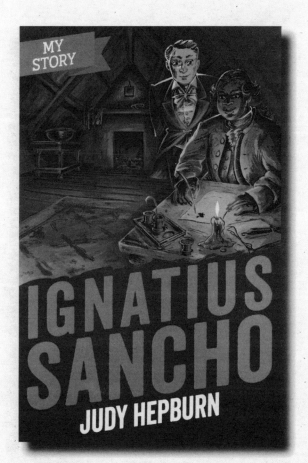

MY
STORY

IGNATIUS
SANCHO

JUDY HEPBURN

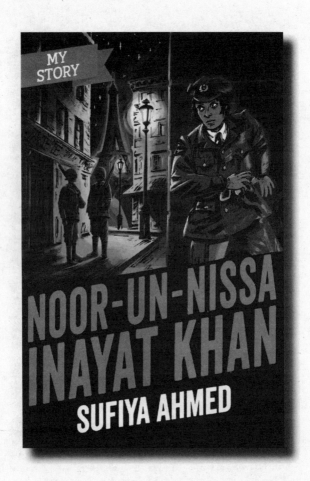

MY STORY

NOOR-UN-NISSA INAYAT KHAN

SUFIYA AHMED

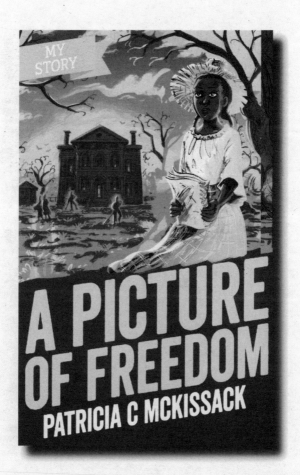

MY
STORY

A PICTURE
OF FREEDOM

PATRICIA C MCKISSACK

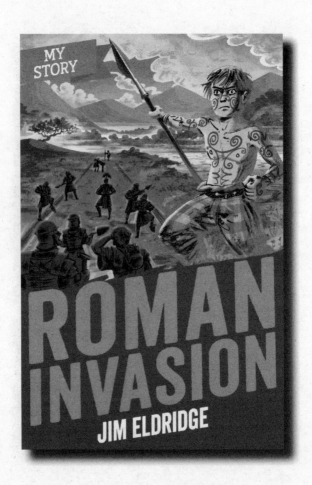

MY
STORY

ROMAN
INVASION

JIM ELDRIDGE

MY
STORY

VICTORIA

ANNA KIRWAN

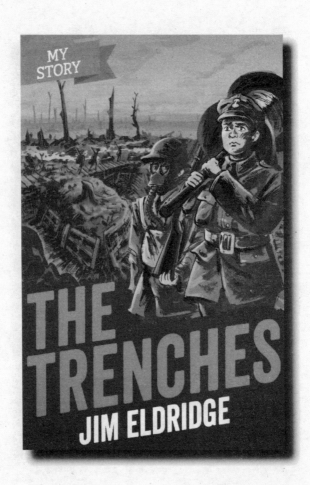

MY
STORY

THE
MAYFLOWER

KATHRYN LASKY

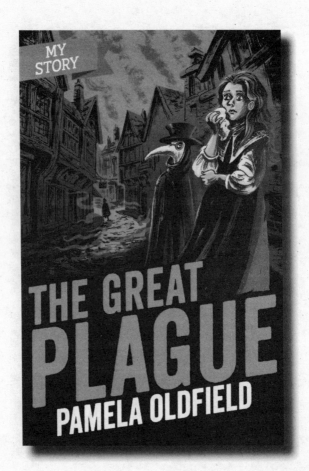

MY
STORY

THE GREAT
PLAGUE

PAMELA OLDFIELD

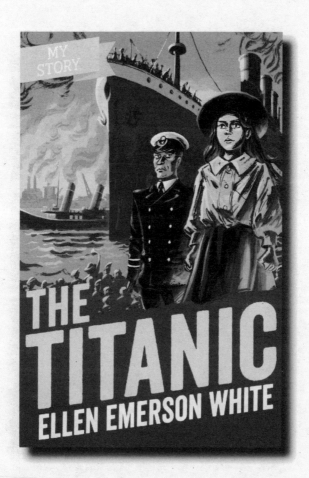

MY STORY

THE TITANIC

ELLEN EMERSON WHITE

MY
STORY

BLITZ

VINCE CROSS